BOOKS BY ISHMAEL REED

NOVELS
Flight to Canada
The Last Days of Louisiana Red
Mumbo Jumbo
Yellow Back Radio Broke Down
The Free-Lance Pallbearers

POETRY
Chattanooga
Conjure

EDITOR
19 Necromancers from Now
Yardbird Reader (editorial director)

FLIGHT TO CANADA

FLIGHT
TO CANADA

ISHMAEL
REED

 *RANDOM HOUSE NEW YORK*

All rights reserved under International and Pan-American Copyright
Conventions. Published in the United States by Random House, Inc.,
New York, and simultaneously in Canada by Random House of Canada
Limited, Toronto.

Library of Congress Cataloging in Publication Data
Reed, Ishmael, 1938–
Flight to Canada.
1. United States—History—Civil War, 1861–1865—
Fiction. I. Title.
PZ4.R323Fl [PS3568.E365] 813'.5'4 76–15598
ISBN 0–394–48754–0

Manufactured in the United States of America

98765432

For Skeleton Fixer

"Evil dogs us."
—JAMES BERTOLINO

Part I
NAUGHTY HARRIET

Flight to Canada

Dear Massa Swille:
What it was?
I have done my Liza Leap
& am safe in the arms
of Canada, so
Ain't no use your Slave
Catchers waitin on me
At Trailways
I won't be there

I flew in non-stop
Jumbo jet this A.M. Had
Champagne
Compliments of the Cap'n
Who announced that a
Runaway Negro was on the
Plane. Passengers came up
And shook my hand
& within 10 min. I had
Signed up for 3 anti-slavery
Lectures. Remind me to get an
Agent

Traveling in style
Beats craning your neck after
The North Star and hiding in

Bushes anytime, Massa
Besides, your Negro dogs
Of Hays & Allen stock can't
Fly

By now I s'pose that
Yellow Judas Cato done tole
You that I have snuck back to
The plantation 3 maybe 4 times
Since I left the first time

Last visit I slept in
Your bed and sampled your
Cellar. Had your prime
Quadroon give me
She-Bear. Yes, yes

You was away at a
Slave auction at Ryan's Mart
In Charleston & so I knowed
You wouldn't mind
Did you have a nice trip, Massa?

I borrowed your cotton money
to pay for my ticket & to get
Me started in this place called
Saskatchewan Brrrrrrr!
It's cold up here but least
Nobody is collaring hobbling gagging
Handcuffing yoking chaining & thumbscrewing
You like you is they hobby horse

The Mistress Ms. Lady
Gived me the combination
To your safe, don't blame
The feeble old soul, Cap'n
I told her you needed some

More money to shop with &
You sent me from Charleston
To get it. Don't worry
Your employees won't miss
It & I accept it as a
Down payment on my back
Wages

I must close now
Massa, by the time you gets
This letter old Sam will have
Probably took you to the
Deep Six

That was rat poison I left
In your Old Crow

Your boy
Quickskill

1

Little did I know when I wrote the poem "Flight to Canada" that there were so many secrets locked inside its world. It was more of a reading than a writing. Everything it said seems to have caught up with me. Other things are running away. The black in my hair is running away. The bad spirits who were in me left a long time ago. The devil who was catching up with me is slipping behind and losing ground. What a war it was!

Lincoln. Harriet Beecher Stowe. Douglass. Jeff Davis and Lee. Me, 40s, and Stray Leechfield. Robin and Judy. Princess Quaw Quaw Tralaralara. Mammy Barracuda. Cato the Graffado.* Yankee Jack. Pompey. Bangalang. It affected us all one way or the other.

"So you're the little woman who started the big war," Lincoln was supposed to have said. Received Harriet Beecher Stowe in the White House, only to have her repay his courtesy by spreading the rumor that he was illiterate. They were always spreading rumors about Lincoln. That he and his son Todd were drunks. That Mrs. Lincoln was mad. That he was a womanizer. That his mother Nancy Hanks was a slut. The Confederates said that he was a "nigger." Who is to say what is fact and what is fiction?

*Sometimes spelled Griffado.

Old Harriet. Naughty Harriet. Accusing Lord Byron of pornography. She couldn't take to Lincoln. She liked Nobility. Curious. The woman who was credited with ruining the Planters was a toady to Nobility, just as they were. Strange, history. Complicated, too. It will always be a mystery, history. New disclosures are as bizarre as the most bizarre fantasy.

Harriet caught some of it. She popularized the American novel and introduced it to Europe. Uncle Tom's Cabin. *Writing is strange, though. That story caught up with her. The story she "borrowed" from Josiah Henson. Harriet only wanted enough money to buy a silk dress. The paper mills ground day and night. She'd read Josiah Henson's book. That Harriet was alert.* The Life of Josiah Henson, Formerly a Slave. *Seventy-seven pages long. It was short, but it was his. It was all he had. His story. A man's story is his gris-gris, you know. Taking his story is like taking his gris-gris. The thing that is himself. It's like robbing a man of his Etheric Double. People pine away. It baffles the doctors the way some people pine away for no reason. For no reason? Somebody has made off with their Etheric Double, has crept into the hideout of themselves and taken all they found there. Human hosts walk the streets of the cities, their eyes hollow, the spirit gone out of them. Somebody has taken their story.*

Josiah Henson went away and fell in love with wood. Nobody could take his wood. His walnut boards. He took his walnut boards to England and exhibited them at the Crystal Palace. Met the young Queen Victoria.

Nobody could take away his Dawn, his settlement in Canada.

Harriet gave Josiah credit in her The Key to Uncle Tom's Cabin. *What was the key to her Cabin? Strange woman, that Harriet. Josiah would never have thought of waging a plot-toting suit against her. Couldn't afford one anyway. Besides, he was bad at figures. His Dawn went broke because he was trusting and bad at figures. It's unfortunate when a man's Dawn goes broke, leaving him hopeless and frustrated. When I see those two men in* The New York Times *in a booth in a fancy restau-*

rant—two bulb-faced jaded men, sitting there, rich as Creole Candy, discussing the money they're going to make from the musical version of Uncle Tom's Cabin, and they have those appetizers in front of them and three kinds of wine—when I see that, and when I see their agent in National Era swimming in the ocean with his chow dog, I wonder why won't the spirits go out to Long Island and touch him. Touch him for what he did to Josiah Henson. Touch him like they touched Harriet.

Harriet paid. Oh yes, Harriet paid. When you take a man's story, a story that doesn't belong to you, that story will get you. Harriet made enough money on someone else's plot to buy thousands of silk dresses and a beautiful home, "One of those spacious frame mansions of bland and hospitable mien which the New England joiners knew so well how to build." A Virginia plantation in New England.

Henson had to sell Dawn, his settlement, to pay his creditors. Is there no sympathy in Nature? Dawn, that's a pretty name. Are people lost because the gods have deserted when they said they never would? They promised they never would. Are they concealing themselves to spite the mean-minded, who are too unimaginative to recognize the new forms they've given themselves? Are they rebuking us for our stupidity? They are mean and demanding. They want to be fed. But before you can feed you have to recognize. They told Josiah Henson to behave with "gentlemanly dignity." But the common people knew. Guede knew. Guede is here. Guede is in New Orleans. Guede got people to write parodies and minstrel shows about Harriet. How she made all that money. Black money. That's what they called it. The money stained her hands.

When Lord Byron came out of the grave to get her, the cartoon showed Harriet leaving her dirty stains all over Byron's immaculate and idealized white statue. Did Josiah Henson do this? The man so identified with Uncle Tom that his home in Dresden, Canada, is called Uncle Tom's Museum? Did Tom have the power the Brazilians say he has? Does he know "roots"? Umbanda. Pretos Velhos, Pai Tomas, Pai Tomas. The "curer." Did Tom make Byron's ghost rise out of his undead *burial place of Romance and strangle Harriet's reputation, so that one biographer entitled a chapter dealing with the scandal "Catastrophe"? Do the old African and Indian gods walk the land as the old one said they would, too proud to reveal themselves to the mean-minded? The mean-minded who won't pay attention. Too hard-headed and mean-minded to see. Harriet's HooDoo book. "I was an instrument of the Lord." HooDoo writing.*

Do the lords still talk? Do the lords still walk? Are they writing this book? Will they go out to Long Island and touch these men who were musing in the restaurant about the money they were going to make on the musical comedy Uncle Tom's Cabin? *Will they get the old mummy grip?*

Harriet said that Byron was fucking his sister. She said that she'd gotten it from her friend Lady Byron, who she felt had been slandered by Countess Guiccioli, Byron's last mistress and the tramp of the Tuilleries Gardens. Harriet accused Byron and his half-sister Augusta Leigh of sharing lustful embrace. Is that why Harriet, the spinster, referred to Lord Byron as a "brilliant seductive genius"? Watch what you put down on the page, Harriet. Did Harriet want to trade places with Augusta Leigh and transform Byron into her brother, Henry? History sure is complicated, or can you, like Stray Leechfield, cash your way out of history?

Why isn't Edgar Allan Poe recognized as the principal biographer of that strange war? Fiction, you say? Where does fact begin and fiction leave off? Why does the perfectly rational, in its own time, often sound like mumbo-jumbo? Where did it leave off for Poe, prophet of a civilization buried alive, where, according to witnesses, people were often whipped for no reason. No reason? Will we ever know, since there are so few traces left of the civilization the planters called "the fairest civilization the sun ever shown upon," and the slaves called "Satan's Kingdom." Poe got it all down. Poe says more in a few stories than all of the volumes by historians. Volumes about that war. The Civil War. The Spirit War. Douglass, Tubman and Bibb all believing in omens, consulting conjure and carrying unseen amulets on their persons. Lincoln, the American Christ, who died on Good Friday. Harriet saying that God wrote Uncle Tom's Cabin. *Which God? Some gods will mount any horse. Even the spinster schoolteacher crawling like an animal from the sightseeing bus toward an Umbanda temple with no a priori beliefs, as they say.*

Dressed in white planter's pants, white waistcoat and white shoes, Raven Quickskill dines alone at the end of a long white Virginia table.

He has just consumed a good old Southern meal of plum pudding, wild duck, oyster soup and Madeira wine, the kind of meal Kentucky generals used to sup at Jeff Davis' "white house" in Montgomery before the South was reduced to corn bread and molasses. All of the boarders had left the Castle for the weekend. All fifty of them. Craftsmen from all over the South: blacksmiths, teachers, sculptors, writers. Uncle Robin had become exultant when Quickskill first made the suggestion. He hadn't been able to figure his way out of his inheritance.

He and Judy traveled a lot. Now they were in the Ashanti Holy Land. Their last trip out they had brought back some serpents. They had given Quickskill the whole first floor of their Castle. It was airy and had big spacious rooms. Mountains, meadows, and the Atlantic Ocean could be seen through the windows. Quickskill would write Uncle Robin's story in such a way that, using a process the old curers used, to lay hands on the story would be lethal to the thief. That way his Uncle Robin would have the protection that Uncle Tom (Josiah Henson) didn't. (Or did he merely use another technique to avenge his story? Breathing life into Byron.)

Raven has the Richmond newspaper spread out in front of him. Princess Quaw Quaw has been arrested carrying a fifteen-foot balance pole, two American flags at each end, while walking on the steel cables of the Golden Gate Bridge. In the photo, crowds were hurling pellets at the officers for interfering with Quaw Quaw's act. She was beginning to become an international event, and the media speculated about her every action. She was becoming the female Blondin, a characterization she resented. "Why don't they call him the male Quaw Quaw Tralaralara?" she once protested in an interview.

This is not to say that she became a media bug. She insisted on her privacy and occasionally there were photos of her wandering about her husband's yacht, nude, wearing sunglasses, as he docked off Trinidad, Majorca or Sausalito.

The note she had left Quickskill on the dresser of the Eagle Hotel had read merely, "Gone South," with her signature scrawled underneath.

He had sent a note to her in care of her agent:

Dear Quaw Quaw Wherever or Whoever:
        Maybe one day people of your class will realize that people of my class must grovel, worm and root our way through life fending off the bad birds so we've little time to take those we love under our wing. And that we become like mythical Goofus birds, invented by lumbermen I think, who fly backwards and build their nests upside down. We get smashed and our endings are swift.

And she wrote back:

Dear Raven:
        And I thought our people were bad, worshipping Bears, Turtles, Ravens, Coyotes and Eagles, but your people worship any old thing or make an "object of reverence" of just about any "new things," as in that HooDoo expression you once taught me, "Only Ghosts Hate New Things," and then that morning I saw you, in our berth, on the steamer, Lake Erie mumbling before it, the typewriter was sitting there and seemed to be crouched like a black frog with white clatter for teeth. You thought I was asleep.

And it went on that way until one day she signed a letter "See you soon." And that was that. She'd be back. She always came back. And they always had quarrels about "the human condition," as her Columbia Professors would say.

"Flight to Canada" was the problem. It made him famous but had also tracked him down. It had pointed to where he, 40s and Stray Leechfield were hiding. It was their bloodhound, this poem "Flight to Canada." It had tracked him down just as his name had. The name his mother gave him before she went away into the Fog Woman. It had dogged him. "Evil Dogs Us." Yes, indeed. His poem flew just as his name had flown. Raven. A scavenger to some, a bringer of new light to others. The one who makes war against the Ganooks of this world. As quick on his opponents as a schooner on a slaver. "Flight to Canada" had given him enough mint to live on. "Flight to Canada" had taken him all the way to the White House, where he shook hands with Abe the Player, as history would call him.

He had never gotten along with Uncle Robin in slavery, but away from slavery they were the best of friends. He would try to live up to the confidence Robin had in him by writing a good book. "You put witchery on the word," Robin said. He would try to put witchery on the word.

Uncle Robin had turned down an offer from Jewett and Company of Boston's best-known writer and had put his story in the hands of Quickskill: "Now you be careful with my story," Robin said. "Treat that story as precious as old Swille treated his whips." They both knew what that meant.

Bangalang came into the room from the kitchen. She was about to leave to return to the Frederick Douglass Houses where she and her husband lived. His carriage was outside waiting for her.

"Is there anything else I can get for you?" she asked Quickskill.

"No," he said, and then, "Bangalang?"

"Yes, Quickskill?"

She had gotten a little grey. They had all gotten a little grey.

"Do you hear from Mammy Barracuda and Cato the Graffado?"

"Last I heard, she sang before the last reunion of Confederate Soldiers. They—"

"What happened, Bangalang?" She'd begun to laugh.

"She sang a chorus from 'Dixie.' Well, I have to tell you when she got to those lines that go 'Will run away—Missus took a decline, oh / Her face was de color ob bacon-rine-oh!', the old soldiers took Mammy on their shoulders and marched her out from the convention hall. Cato was leading the parade like a cheerleader, I'm telling you. Well, if you need something else, there's an apple pie in the kitchen." She turned and walked out.

Curious. Even in the Confederate anthem there was a belle fading away and losing her color. What was this fascination with declining belles in the South? What was the South all about? I'll have to include all of this in my story, Quickskill thought.

Quickskill drank his coffee. He had a swell. His belly was up again. He spent so much time in thought, he forgot about his stomach. That was the writing business all right. He'd been writing since he could remember; his "Flight to Canada" was to him what blacks were to old Abe.

"Abe Lincoln's last card or Rouge et Noir" was the caption under the wood engraving printed in *Punch* magazine. It showed Lincoln beating a Confederate with his ace of spades. Inside the card's black spade was the grinning Negro. The engraving was by Sir John Tenniel, a Royalist. He'd have to write all of this in Robin's story.

Raven was the first one of Swille's slaves to read, the first to write and the first to run away. Master Hugh, the bane of Frederick Douglass, said, "If you give a nigger an inch, he'll take an ell. If you teach him how to read, he'll want to know how to write. And this accomplished, he'll be running away with himself."

Master Hugh could have taught Harriet Beecher Stowe a thing or two.

2

People don't know when the Swilles came to Virginia, and the Swilles ain't talkin. Perhaps that's why they live behind those great gates one reaches through mossy land and swamps full of so many swine that Swilles' land has been named Swine'rd, Virginia.

According to the family records we do have, we know that the first Swille, a zealous slave trader, breeder and planter, was "indescribably deformed." He did his business from the tower of a Castle he built on his grounds, said to be the very replica of King Arthur's in the Holy City of Camelot, the Wasp's Jerusalem, the great Fairy City of the old Feudal Order, of the ancient regime; of knights, ladies, of slaves; of jousting; of toasting; Camelot, a land of endless games. Seeing who could pull the Sword out of an anvil of iron. Listening to the convoluted prophecies of Merlin the Druid. Listening to Arthur and his knights, so refined and noble that they launched a war against the Arabs for the recovery of an *objet d'art,* yet treated their serfs like human plows, de-budding their women at will; torturing and witchifying the resistance with newfangled devices. Dracula, if you recall, was a count.

Arthur was England's Alfonzo of the Kongo, the Pope's native ruler who saw to it that the "heathen art" was destroyed.

He was John Wallace of Hydaburg, the Christian native who persuaded the Tlingits to "cut down and burn" the great totem poles of Klinkwan. Arthur, whose father, Uther, according to Tennyson, was "dark," even "well-nigh black" and so "sweet" some took him to be "less a man."

Arthur made war against the Saxons and the old Druid gods who are depicted as monsters in his Romance. His descendants came to his America and made war against the gods of "Indians" and Africans.

Camelot became Swille's bible, and one could hear him in the tower, giggling elflike as he came to each new insight; and they heard him dancing as Camelot, a fairy tale to most, became for him an Anglican Grand Design.

After Swille "crossed over," his dream was taken up by Swille II, Rockland Swille, hero of the Battle of Buena Vista in "Mr. Polk's War." This Swille became "afflicted," when he returned to Swine'rd, with an "inexplicable malady." His wife was shut up in a sanitarium after witnessing what became known as "Swille's malady" in the secret books of the old medical library, shelved so far back in the cavernous stacks.

His son, Swille III, was named Arthur because by that time a group of intelligent Virginia Planters had organized a branch of the Circle of the Golden Dawn and one of its notions was that the "Coming of Arthur" was at hand. (In certain books, Jefferson Davis, the President of the Confederacy, also an Anglican, is referred to as "Our Arthur" or "The South's Arthur.") This group of Planters held meetings at a private Richmond club called the Magnolia Baths and was said to have exerted considerable influence during the proceedings of the secret Montgomery Convention where the plans for the Confederacy were drawn.

Arthur Swille received the licentious Hedonist Award for 1850 and was known in London and Paris circles as a gay blade, until he returned to Swine'rd to manage his Family's great fortune after Swille II had mysteriously "pined away."

This Swille, Swille III, Arthur Swille, obeyed no nation's laws and once flogged Queen Victoria, a weekend guest at his

English Country Manor, after a copy of *Uncle Tom's Cabin* turned up in a search of her room.

Others say it was because Victoria refused to sell Swille III a barony; according to insiders, Victoria stuck to her guns, moaning, "Europe is not for sale, Mr. Swille," grunting, "Europe is not for sale, Mr. Swille," as Swille's stud, Jim, brought the lash down upon the red striated back of the Queen of England. A proud day for the British Empire.

Security is stiff on the Swilles' ground. Patrollers, called "paddies" by the slaves, reconnoiter the slave quarters.

Some say it's due to Swille's bitterness about the unfortunate and untimely death of his son, the anthropologist, whose head was returned to him in a box, covered with what a biopsy revealed as cells from a disgruntled crocodile.

The Snake Society went on satellite television to take credit for it, and added an especially grisly sidelight to a most heinous crime by joking that the head was covered with crocodile regurgitation because Mitchell was too rich for the crocodile, and that the crocodile just kinda laid around on the banks these days, wearing Bloomingdale shades, and was calling himself Aldo the Gourmet Crocodile.

It was reported from the Castle that Swille fired a pistol into the television set when he heard that, and in reprisal immediately ordered the execution of the North American crocodile in such a fiendish manner that by 1977 there will be only eighteen North American crocodiles left. Excuse me, twelve.

To add to this general mood of dolor and dread, three slaves—40s, Stray Leechfield and Raven Quickskill—have vanished.

3

The Master's study. Arthur Swille has just completed the push-ups he does after his morning nourishment, two gallons of slave mothers' milk. Uncle Robin, his slave, is standing against the wall, arms folded. He is required to dress up as a Moorish slave to satisfy one of Swille's cravings.

"Robin?"

"Yessir, Massa Swille."

"What are the people down in the quarters saying about those kinks who took off with themselves?"

"Don't get down to the slave village much any more, Massa Swille. After you and Cato the Graffado put out directions that none was to tarry there, I tain't. We were gettin all of our information from Stray Leechfield, the runner, but now that he's . . . well, after he . . ."

"Yes, you don't have to say it, Robin. He's gone. Stray Leechfield, 40s and [voice drops] Quickskill. They contracted *Drapetomania,* as that distinguished scientist Dr. Samuel Cartwright described in that book you read to me . . ."

"*Dysaethesia Aethipica,* Mr. Swille?"

"Exactly, Robin, that disease causing Negroes to run away. Of course, I'm not a sentimentalist. I won't sleep until they've returned. I mean, I'm the last man to go against science, and if a slave is sick, then he must be rejuvenated—but I just can't permit anyone to run over me like that. The other slaves will get ideas. So, even though they're sick—they must be returned."

"But suppose they paid you off. Would you try to recover even then?"

"Look, Robin, if they'd came to me and if they'd asked to buy themselves, perhaps we could have arranged terms. But they didn't; they furtively pilfered themselves. Absconded. They have committed a crime, and no amount of money they send me will rectify the matter. I'd buy all the niggers in the South before I'd accept a single dime for or from them . . . Quickskill, I'll never be able to figure out. Why, he ate in the house and was my trusted bookkeeper. I allowed him to turn the piano pages when we had performers in the parlor, even let him wear a white wig—and he'd give all of this up. Well," he said, pounding on the top of his desk, "they won't get away with it. One thing my father told me: never yield a piece of property. Not to a man, not to the State. Before he died, that's what he told me and my brothers."

Dressed in his robes, Swille reaches out his hand, which embraces a wineglass. Uncle Robin walks over to the spirits cabinet, returns and pours him a gobletful, goes back to his place. Uncle Robin knows his place—his place in the shadows.

"Robin, what have you heard about this place up North, I think they call it Canada?" Swille says, eying Robin slyly.

"Canada. I do admit I have heard about the place from time to time, Mr. Swille, but I loves it here so much that . . . that I would never think of leaving here. These rolling hills. Mammy singing spirituals in the morning before them good old biscuits. Watching 'Sleepy Time Down South' on the Late Show. That's my idea of Canada. Most assuredly, Mr. Swille, this my Canada. You'd better believe it."

"Uncle Robin, I'm glad to hear you say that. Why, I don't know what I'd do without you. I can always count on you not to reveal our little secret. Traveling around the South for me, carrying messages down to the house slaves, polishing my boots and drawing my bath water. All of these luxuries. Robin, you make a man feel like . . . well, like a God."

"Thank you, Massa Swille. I return the compliment. It's such a honor to serve such a mellifluous, stunning and elegant man as yourself, Massa Swille; indeed an honor. Why . . . why, you could be President if you wanted to."

"I toyed with the idea, Robin. But my brothers made me think of the Family. It would be a disgrace to the Swilles if I ever stooped so low as to offer myself to this nation. I'm afraid, Robin, that that office is fit only for rapscallions, mobocrats, buckrahs, coonskinners and second-story men. Before Grand-dad died, they elected that Irishman Andrew Jackson, a cut-up and a barroom brawler, to office—why, I remained in exile during his entire term. Refused even to speak the language, spoke French for those years. It was only after Dad died that I returned to manage this land."

"You're a very busy man, Mr. Swille. The presidency would only be a waste of time for you."

There's a knock on the door. Mammy Barracuda enters. "Arthur," then, noticing Uncle Robin, "Oh, I mean Massa Swille."

"Yes, Barracuda?"

Barracuda has a silk scarf tied about her head. A black velvet dress. She wears a diamond crucifix on her bosom. It's so heavy she walks with a stoop. Once she went into the fields and the sun reflected on her cross so, two slaves were blinded.

"It's your wife, Ms. Swille, sir. She say she tired of being a second-class citizen and she say she don't want to feed herself no mo. She say it's anti-suffragette. She say she shouldn't have to exert herself to feed herself and she say she wont to be fed extravenous, I mean, fed intravenous, somethin. Grumph. When she do get out of bed, we have to rock her in the rocking chair. We have to wash her feet and then empty her spoils. The room ain't been aired out in months. She say she boycott somethin. Humph!"

"If it isn't one thing, it's another. You mean she won't eat at all?"

"She told me to mail this letter. I thought I'd show it to you. See what you thought about it before I mailed it."

"Very thoughtful of you, Barracuda."

He takes the letter, opens it.

"What you lookin at?"

"I was just admiring your new apron, Mammy Barracuda, that's all," Uncle Robin says.

"Better be. Humph. Grumph."

"Destroy this letter, Barracuda. A one-year subscription to that *National Era* which carried the work by that fanatical Beecher woman."

"I will burn it first chance I get, Massa Swille. What about him?"

"I trust Robin second only to you, Barracuda. Lying curled up fetuslike in your lap is worth a hundred shrinks on Park Avenue."

"Humph. Whew. Wheeew," utters Barracuda, of whom it once was rumored "she stared a man to death," as she goes out.

"Wonderful old soul, Mammy Barracuda."

"You can second that twice for me, Massa Swille."

"What's that, Robin?"

"That part about her being a wonderful old soul. You can second that twice for me."

4

There's a knock at the door. It's Moe, the white house slave —Mingy Moe, as the mammies in the kitchen call him. He looks like an albino: tiny pink pupils, white Afro.

"Sorry to disturb you, Master Swille, but Abe Lincoln, the President of the so-called Union, is outside in the parlor waiting to see you. He's fiddling around and telling corny jokes, shucking the shud and husking the hud. I told him that you were scheduled to helicopter up to Richmond to shake your butt at the Magnolia Baths tonight, but he persists. Says, 'The very survival of the Union is at stake.' "

"Hand me my jacket, Uncle Robin," Swille says as he stands in the middle of the room.

"Which one do you wont, suh—the one with the spangly fritters formal one or the silvery-squilly festooned street jacket?"

"Give me the spangly one." Turning to Moe, Swille says, "Now, Moe, you tell this Lincoln gentleman that he won't be able to stay long. Before I fly up to Richmond, I have to check on my investments all over the world."

"Yessir, Mr. Swille."

Momentarily, Lincoln, Gary Cooper-awkward, fidgeting with his stovepipe hat, humble-looking, imperfect—a wart here and there—craw and skuttlecoat, shawl, enters the room. "Mr. Swille, it's a pleasure," he says, extending his hand to Swille, who sits behind a desk rumored to have been owned by Napoleon III. "I'm a small-time lawyer and now I find myself in the room of the mighty, why—"

"Cut the yokel-dokel, Lincoln, I don't have all day. What's on your mind?" Swille rejects Lincoln's hand, at which Lincoln stares, hurt.

"Yokel-dokel? Why, I don't get you, Mr. Swille."

"Oh, you know—log-cabin origin. That's old and played out. Why don't you get some new speech writers? Anyway, you're the last man I expected to see down here. Aren't you supposed to be involved in some kind of war? Virginia's off limits to your side, isn't it? Aren't you frightened, man?"

"No, Mr. Swille. We're not frightened because we have a true cause. We have a great, a noble cause. Truth is on our side, marching to the clarion call. We are in the cause of the people. It is a people's cause. This is a great, noble and people period in the history of our great Republic. We call our war the Civil War, but some of the fellows think we ought to call it the War Between the States. You own fifty million dollars' worth of art, Mr. Swille. What do you think we ought to call it?"

"I don't feel like naming it, Lanky—and cut the poppy-cock."

"Lincoln, sir."

"Oh yes, Lincoln. Well, look, Lincoln, I don't want that war to come up here because, to tell you the truth, I'm not the least bit interested in that war. I hate contemporary politics and probably will always be a Tory. Bring back King George. Why would a multinational like myself become involved in these queer crises? Why, just last week I took a trip abroad and was appallingly and disturbingly upset and monumentally offended by the way the Emperor of France was scoffing at this . . . this nation, as you call it. They were snickering about your general unkempt, hirsute and bungling appearance—bumping into things and carrying on. And your speeches. What kind of gibberish are they? Where were you educated, in the rutabaga patch? Why don't you put a little pizazz in your act, Lanky? Like Davis . . . Now that Davis is as nit as a spit with his satin-embroidered dressing case, his gold tweezers and Rogers & Sons strap. He's just bananas about Wagner and can converse in German, French and even that bloody Mexican patois. Kindly toward the 'weak' races, as he referred to them in that superb speech he made before the Senate criticizing Secretary of State Seward and other celebrities for financing that, that . . . maniac, John Brown. And when he brought in that savage, Black Hawk, on the steamboat *Winnebago,* he treated the primitive overlord with the respect due an ethnic celebrity. You can imagine the Americans taunting this heathen all decked out in white deerskins. Davis' slaves are the only ones I know of who take mineral baths, and when hooped skirts became popular he gave some to the slave women, and when this made it awkward for them to move through the rows of cotton, he widened the rows."

"That's quite impressive, Mr. Swille. I have a worthy adversary."

Swille, smirking and squinting, flicks the ashes from a cigar given him by the King of Belgium. "An intellectual. What an intellectual. Loggerhead turtles? Oysters? Hogarth? Optics? Anything you want to know, Davis's got the answer. And his beautiful wife. More brilliant than most men. As aristocratic as Eugénie, wife of my good friend Imperial Majesty Napoleon Bonaparte III. I was having dinner with her just a few weeks ago. You know, she's the daughter of the Count of Montijo and the Duke of Peneranda. Men who like nothing but the best. I call her Gennie, since we move in the same circles. Why, I'm thinking about refurbishing the Morocco Club in New York—just no place for the royal ones to go any more. We were eating, and she turned to me and asked why Du Chaillur searched for the primitive missing link in Africa when one had shambled into the Capitol from the jungles of the Midwest."

Lincoln looks puzzled. "I don't get it, Mr. Swille."

"She was talking about you, silly. They're calling you the Illinois Ape. Eugénie's a brilliant conversationalist. But Varina Davis has it over her. Those glittering supper parties at the Montgomery White House—and did you see the carriage she bought Jeff? Imported it from New Orleans. Yes indeed, from New Orleans. Almost as good as mine. Upholstered in watered blue silk. Can't you see those two representing the . . . the Imperial Empire of the Confederate States of Europe in London? They might even make him a knight—Sir Jefferson Davis. I can see it all now. And then upon their return, a ticker-tape parade down Broadway, with clerks leaning out of office windows shouting, Long Live Jeff. Long Live Varina. Long Live Jeff. Long Live Varina. The Duke and Duchess of Alabama. What a man. What a man. A prince. One of my friends recently visited this six-plus-foot tall specimen and said he just felt like stripping and permitting this eagle-eyed, blade-nosed, creamy Adonis to abuse him and . . . [pant, pant] humiliate him."

"Come again, Mr. Swille?"

"Oh, Abe, you're so green. Green as jade in a cocaine vision."

"Mr. Swille, mind if we change the subject?"

"We have a delightful life down here, Abe. A land as Tennyson says 'In which it all seemed always afternoon. All round the coast the languid air did swoon. Here are cool mosses deep, and thro the stream the long-leaved flowers weep, and from the craggy ledge the poppy hang in sleep.' Ah. Ah. 'And sweet it is to dream of Fatherland. Of child, and wife and slave. Delight our souls with talk of Knightly deeds. Walking about the gardens and the halls.' And, Abe, a man like you can have a soft easy hustle down here. You could be walking around and wallowing in these balmy gardens and these halls. The good life. Breakfast in a dress coat. Exotic footbaths. Massages three times a day. And what we call down here a 'siesta.' Niggers fanning you. A fresh bouquet of flowers and a potent julep delivered to your room. Roses. Red roses. Yellow roses. White roses. We can bring back the 'days that were.' Just fancy yourself the Earl of Lincoln, or Count Abe. Or Marquis Lincoln. Marquis Lincoln of Springfield. You could have this life, Lincoln." He goes to the window and draws back the curtains. There is a view of the hills of Virginia. "It's all bare now, Lincoln. But we will build that city. From here to as far as the eye can see will be great castles with spires and turrets. We can build one for you, Lincoln. Sir Lincoln."

"I'm afraid I wouldn't like it down here, Mr. Swille. I'm just a mudfish. I don't yen for no fancy flies."

"Think about it, Lincoln. You can take an hour and a half putting on your clothes down here. Why . . . why . . . I'm thinking about taking up Meditative Transcendentalism. I've sent to India for a Swami. You know, you may not be so lucky in the next election year. If it hadn't been for those Hoosiers and Suckers and other rags and patches who packed the Wigwam, you'd be back in your law office in Springfield. Their conduct was disgraceful. Why, I had to tell the networks not to carry it. They hollered you the nomination. Steam whistles. Hotel gongs. Comanches! Liquor flowing like Babylon. Not even top-shelf, but Whiskey Skin, Jersey Lightning and Brandy Smash."

"The boys were just cuttin up, Mr. Swille, just jerking the goose bone."

"And then bribing the delegates with Hoboken cigars and passes to quiz shows. Washington, Jefferson and Monroe must be howling in their chains. And that lunatic wife of yours. Must she dress like that? She looks like a Houston and Bowery streetwalker who eats hero sandwiches and chews bubble gum. Why does she wear that brunette bouffant and those silver high-heel boots? She looks like a laundromat attendant. Old frowzy dough-faced thing. Queens accent. Ever think about taking her to the Spa? And why does she send those midnight telegrams to the *Herald Tribune* after drinking God knows what? And there's another thing I've been meaning to ask you, Mr. Lincoln."

"What is that, Mr. Swille?"

"Do you think it appropriate for the President of the

United States to tell such lewd jokes to the boys in the telegraph room? The one about the cow and the farmer. The traveling salesmen and the milkmaid. The whole scabrous repertoire."

"How did you know that, Mr. Swille?"

"Never you mind. And you think it's befitting your exalted office to go about mouthing the sayings of that hunchback Aesop? No wonder the Confederate cartoonists are beginning to depict you as a nigger. They're calling you a Black Republican down here, and I've heard some weird talk from the planters. Some strange ugly talk. I want you to read that book they're all reading down here. Uncle Robin! Give Lanky that book they're all reading down here."

Robin goes to the shelf. *"Idylls of the King,* Mr. Swille?"

"Yes, that's the one."

Robin removes the book from the shelf and gives it to Lincoln.

"This book tells you about aristocratic rule, Lincoln. How to deal with inferiors. How to handle the help. How the chief of the tribes is supposed to carry himself. You're not the steadiest man for the job; you'd better come on and get this Camelot if you know what's good for you. You, too, can have a wife who is jaundiced and prematurely buried. Skin and bones. Got her down to seventy-five pounds. She's a good sufferer but not as good as Vivian, she . . ." Swille gazes toward the oil portrait of his sister.

"What . . . Anything wrong?" Lincoln says, beginning to rise from his chair.

Robin starts toward Swille.

"No, nothing. Where was I, Robin?"

"You were telling Mr. Lincoln about Camelot, sir."

"Look, Lincoln, if you don't want to be a duke, it's up to you. I need a man like you up in my Canadian mills. You can be a big man up there. We treat the Canadians like coons. I know you used to chop wood. You can be a powerful man up there. A powerful man. Why, you can be Abe of the Yukon. Why don't you resign and call it quits, Lincoln? You won't have to sneak into the Capitol disguised any more. What ya say, pal?"

"Look, Mr. Swille, maybe I ought to tell you why I came down here. Then we can cut this as short and sweet as an old woman's dance."

"All right, Abe. But before you tell me, look, Abe, I don't want to get into politics, but, well, why did you up and join such a grotesque institution as that party that . . ."

"We call ourselves the Republican party, Mr. Swille, but don't look at me. I didn't name it."

"A far-out institution if there ever was one. Free Soilers, whacky money people, Abolitionists. Can't you persuade some of those people to wear a tie? Transcendentalists, Free Lovers, Free Farmers, Whigs, Know-Nothings, and those awful Whitmanites always running about hugging things."

"Look, Mr. Swille," Lincoln says in his high-pitched voice, "I didn't come here to discuss my party, I came to discuss how we could win this war, Mr. Swille; end this conflict," he says, pounding the table. "We are in a position to give the South its death-knell blow."

" 'Death-knell blow.' There you go again with that cornpone speech, Lincoln. 'Death-knell blow.' Why don't you shave off that beard and stop putting your fingers in your lapels like that. You ought to at least try to polish yourself, man. Go to the theatre. Get some culture. If you don't, I'll have to contact my general; you know, there's always one of our people keeping an eye on things in your . . . your cabinets. Why, under the Crown . . ."

"Now you look here, Mr. Swille. I won't take your threats. I knew it was a mistake to come down here, you . . . you slave-flogging pea-picker."

Arthur Swille, startled, removes his cigar from his mouth.

"Yes, I know what you think of me. I never went to none of that fancy Harvard and don't lounge around Café Society quaffing white wine until three in the afternoon, and maybe my speeches don't contain a lot of Latin, and maybe my anecdotes aren't understated and maybe I ain't none of that cologned

rake sojourning over shrimp cocktails or sitting around in laven-
der knee britches, like a randy shank or a dandy rake.

"I know you make fun of our nation, our war and our
party, Mr. Swille. I know that you hold it against us because
our shirts stick out of our britches and we can't write long
sentences without losing our way, but you wouldn't be sitting
up here in this . . . this Castle if it weren't for the people. The
public people. And the Republic people in this great people
period, and that ain't no pipple papple pablum either, pal."

A train whistle is heard.

"Mr. Swille, listen to your train. That great locomotive
that will soon be stretching across America, bumping cows,
pursued by Indians, linking our Eastern cities with the West
Coast. Who built your trains, Mr. Swille? The people did, Mr.
Swille. Who made you what you are today, Mr. Swille? A swell
titanic titan of ten continents, Mr. Swille. Who worked and
sweated and tilled and toiled and travailed so that you could
have your oil, your industry, Mr. Swille? Why, we did, Mr.
Swille. Who toted and tarried and travestied themselves so that
you could have your many homes, your ships and your buildings
reaching the azure skies? We did, Mr. Swille. Yes, I know I'm
a corn-bread and a catfish-eatin curmudgeon known to sup
some scuppernong wine once in a while, but I will speak my
mind, Mr. Swille. Plain Abe. Honest Abe. And I don't care
how much power you have in Congress, it won't stop me
speaking my mind, and if you say another word about my wife,
Mr. Swille, I'm going to haul off and go you one right upside
your fat head. Don't forget I used to split rails." Lincoln turns
around. "I'm leaving."

Uncle Robin, blinking back tears, applauds Lincoln until
Swille gives him a stern look.

"Hey, wait a minute, come back, Mr. Lincoln, Mr. President."

Lincoln, stunned, stops and slowly turns around.

"You know, I like your style. You're really demanding,
aren't you?" Swille takes the old keys from his right hip and
fastens them to his left. "How's about a drink of Old Crow?"

"Well, I'll stay for a few more minutes, but I warn you, Mr. Swille, if you so much as whisper some calumny and perfidy about my wife, I'm going to belt you one."

"Sure, Mr. President. Sure," Swille says as Lincoln returns to his seat in front of Swille's desk. Swille is at the liquor cabinet reaching for the Old Crow, when, *zing!* a bullet comes from the direction of the window and shatters the bottle. The contents spill to the floor.

"Why, I'll be . . ." Swille says, staring at the pieces of glass on the floor. Lincoln and Uncle Robin are under the desk. Moe, the white house slave, rushes in. "Massa Swille, Massa Swille, the Confederates are outside whooping it up and breaking Mr. Lincoln's carriage. We hid Mr. Lincoln's party down in the wine cellar until the episode passed, and do you know what, Mr. Swille? Somebody has drunk up all the wine."

"Somebody has drunk up all the wine!" Swille and Uncle Robin say.

"Uncle Robin, give me the telephone. I want to call Lee."

Uncle Robin obliges, tiptoeing across the room, grinning widely.

"I don't want any of that grey trash snooping about my door," Swille says, frowning.

Outside, rebel yells can be heard.

"Hello? Give me that Lee . . . Well, I don't care if he is at the front, tell him to bring his ass away from the front. This is Arthur Swille speaking . . ." To Lincoln, Moe and Uncle Robin, "That got em."

"Hello, Lee? What's the big idea of your men come busting up to my place and annoying my guests? I told your boss, Jeff Davis, to keep that war off of my property . . . Why, you impertinent scoundrel." Hand over the phone, he mimics Lee to the trio in the room, "Says extraordinary emergency supersedes the right to privacy enjoyed by the individual no matter what station in life the individual may hold . . . Look, you little runt, if you don't get those men off my property, I'll, I'll . . . My father's dead, I'm running this thing now. I don't care how long you've known the family—my brothers and Ms. Anne and me are running things now . . .

"Who's up here? Why, the nerve. For your information, Mr. Abraham Lincoln is up here,"

Lincoln tries to shush Swille, but Swille signals him that it doesn't matter.

"You'll do no such thing." Hand over the phone, to Lincoln, "Says he's coming up here to arrest you . . .

"Look, Lee, if you don't get those men off my property I'm going to create an energy crisis and take back my railroads, and on top of that I'll see that the foreign countries don't recognize you. And if that's not all, I'll take back my gold. Don't forget; I control the interest rates . . .

"Now that's more like it . . . Now you're whistling 'Dixie' . . . No, I won't tell Davis . . . Forget it . . . That's fine." Turns to Lincoln, "Says he's going to send an escort up here to see to it that your men return safely to your yacht, *The River Queen.* Lee said he was preparing to blow it up but will call it off in deference to your comfort . . ."

Turning back to the phone, "What's that? . . . Oh, you don't have to come up here and play nigger for three days for punishment; anyway, who will run your side of the war? Look, Lee, I got to go now." Hangs up. To trio, "Boy, when you say gold, they jump. And speaking of gold, Mr. President, I'm going to give you some."

"Why, Mr. Swille, now that you mention it," Lincoln says, fidgeting and pushing his feet, "I didn't come all the way through Confederate lines just to pass the time of day. We need some revenue bad. Why, we're as broke as a skeeter's peeter. I'm leaning toward the peace plan originally proposed by Horace Greeley of the New York paper . . . it's called . . . Well, the plan is called . . ." Lincoln reaches into his coat pocket for a piece of paper. "Ah, Mr. Swille, I didn't bring my glasses, would you read it?" Lincoln hands the piece of paper to Swille.

"And cut the formalities, Mr. Swille. You can call me Abe." Lincoln, once again, reaches out for a handshake, but

Swille is too busy reading to notice. Lincoln, embarrassed, puts his hand in his pocket.

Swille takes the paper and examines it. "I . . . well, your writing, your aide's writing, is nearly illegible. Here, Uncle Robin, can you make this out?"

Robin looks at it. "Compensatory Emancipation it says, Massa Swille."

"Compensatory Emancipation, that's it! Sure enough is, Mr. Swille. It goes like this. We buy the war and the slaves are over. No, like this. We buy the slaves. That's it. We buy the slaves or the bondsmen and then they pay the South seven and a half percent interest. No, dog bite it. How did it go? My aides have been going over it with me ever since we started out from *The River Queen.* I got it! We buy up all the slaves and then tell them to go off somewhere. Some place like New Mexico, where nobody's hardly seen a cloud and when they do show up it looks like judgment day, and where the cactus grows as big as eucalyptus trees, where you have to walk two miles to go to the outhouse and then freeze your can off in the cold desert until it's your turn and then the outhouse is so dark you sit on a rattlesnake. Other times I think that maybe they ought to go to the tropics where God made them. You know, I've been reading about this African tribe that lived in the tropics so long they trained mosquitoes to fight their enemies. Fascinating, don't you think? I need that gold bad, Mr. Swille. Whatever I decide, it'll come in handy."

"Sure, sure, Lincoln, I know. You'll decide what's best. I know that the war is even-steven right now, and this gold will help out. I'll take a chance on your little Union. The nerve of that guy Lee. I'm going to take back that necklace I gave Mrs. Jefferson Davis. Why, they can't do that to me. Just for that . . ." Swille goes to his safe, removes some bags of gold and places them on his desk. "That ought to do it, Mr. President, and if you're in need of some more, I'll open up Fort Knox and all that you guys wheelbarrow out in an hour you can have."

"Why, thank you, Mr. Swille. You're a patriotic man. But all of this gold, really, I . . ."

"Take it. Take it. A long-term loan, Lincoln. I'll fix these Confederates. That Lee. Sits on his horse as if he was Caesar or somebody."

"The Confederates are innocent, Mr. Swille. The other day one of them was tipping his hat and curtsying, and one of my snipers plugged him. And in the Chattanooga campaign, Grant tells me that once he was ascending Lookout Mountain and the Confederate soldiers saluted him. 'Salute to the Commanding General,' they were saying."

The men share a chuckle on this one.

"My generals may look like bums, with their blouses unbuttoned and their excessive drinking and their general ragged appearances, but they know how to fight. Why, that Grant gets sick at the sight of the blood and gets mad when you bring up even the subject of war, and he's never read a military treatise —but he can fight. His only notion of warfare is, 'Go where the enemy is and beat hell out of him.' Crude though it may sound, it seems to work."

"You know, Mr. President, I'm beginning to like you. Here, have a Havana. I have three homes there. Ought to come down some time, Mr. President, play some golf, do some sailing on my yacht. Get away from the Capitol."

"Well, I don't know, Mr. Swille. I'd better not leave town with a war going on and all."

"Where did they get the idea that you were some kind of brooding mystic, tragic and gaunt, a Midwest Messiah with hollow cheeks? I was saying to myself, 'How can a smart corporation lawyer like this Lincoln be so way-out.' "

"I keep my mouth shut, Mr. Swille. And when I can't think quick enough I walk over to the window, put my fingers into my lapels, throw my head back and gaze toward the Washington Monument, assuming a somber, grave and sulfurous countenance. It impresses them, and the myths fly."

"You know, Mr. Lincoln, I wish you'd do something about that fugitive-slave law you promised to enforce during the campaign. There are three of my cocoas at large. I'd like to bring them back here. Teach them a lesson for running away. They're giving the rest of the cocoas around here ideas. They're always caucusing, not admitting any of my white slaves or the white staff—they pass codes to one another, and some of them have taken to writing.

"They're in contact, so it seems, with slaves in the rest of the country, through some kind of intricate grapevine, so Cato my graffado tells me. Sometimes he gets blackened-up with them so's they won't know who he's working for. He's slow but faithful. So faithful that he volunteered for slavery, and so dedicated he is to slavery, the slaves voted him all-Slavery. Sent him to General Howard's Civilizing School. You should have heard my son, who was an authority on sables. He said they're so trusting and kindhearted. I sent him to the Congo to check for some possible energy resources, though he told them he was looking for the source of the Nile. They're so trusting.

"He was majoring in some kind of thing called anthropology in one of those experimental colleges. You know the young. First I wanted him to go to Yale, like me. Then I saw that the little stinker had an angle. What a cover. Anthropologists. We used to send priests, but they were too obvious."

"You must be very proud of him, Mr. Swille."

"He was doing well until . . . until these Congo savages captured him and . . . and . . . well."

"Oh, I'm sorry, was he . . . ?"

"You might say that he was killed. But, Mr. President, we all have our trials. An unpleasant subject. A smart one he was, like your Todd. Very inquisitive. It's upon my son's advice that I don't permit any of the employees to use the telephone. I permit Uncle Robin to use it because he's such a simple creature he wouldn't have the thought powers for using it deviously. He's been in the house for so long that he's lost his thirst for pagan ways and is as good a gentleman as you or me."

Lincoln nods, approvingly.

"Why, thank you, Cap'n Swille."

"Don't mention it, Robin. I don't know what I'd do without you. He brings me two gallons of slave women's milk each morning. It keeps me going. He travels all over the South in an airplane, buying supplies for the estate. He's become quite a bargainer and knows about all of the sales . . .

"Of course, I still buy the . . . well, the help. Just got back from Ryan's Mart in Charleston with a boy named Pompey. Does the work of ten niggers. I got him working in the house here. He doesn't say much but is really fast. The boy can serve dinner before it's cooked, beats himself getting up in the morning so that when he goes to the bathroom to shave he has to push his shadow out of the way, and zips about the house like a toy train. I'm really proud of this bargain. Why, on his days off he stands outside of the door, protecting me, like a piece of wood. He can stand there for hours without even blinking an eye. Says he would die if something happens to me. Isn't that right, Uncle Robin? Though he's asp-tongued and speaks in this nasal tone, Pompey is a saint. He doesn't come down to the races, nor does he Camptown; doesn't smoke, drink, cuss or wench, stays up in his room when he's not working, probably contemplating the Scriptures. They don't make them like that any more, Mr. Lincoln. I have a shrewd eye for good property, don't you think, Abe?"

"Well, Mr. Swille, if you've read my campaign literature, you'd know that my position is very clear. What a man does with his property is his business. Of course, I can't help but agree with one of my distinguished predecessors, George Washington, who said, 'There are numbers who would rather facilitate the escape of slaves than apprehend them as runaways.' That law is hard to enforce, Mr. Swille."

Swille rises. "Look, Lincoln, one of them kinks, 40s, wiped me out when he left here. That venerable mahogany took all my guns, slaughtered my livestock and shot the overseer right between the eyes. And the worst betrayal of all was Raven Quickskill, my trusted bookkeeper. Fooled around with my books, so that every time I'd buy a new slave he'd destroy the invoices and I'd have no record of purchase; he was also writing passes and forging freedom papers. We gave him Literacy, the most powerful thing in the pre-technological pre-post-rational age—and what does he do with it? Uses

it like that old Voodoo—that old stuff the slaves mumble
about. Fetishism and grisly rites, only he doesn't need anything but a pen he had shaped out of cock feathers and
chicken claws. Oh, they are bad sables, Mr. Lincoln. They
are bad, bad sables. Not one of them with the charm and
good breeding of Ms. Phyllis Wheatly, who wrote a poem for
the beloved founder of this country, George Washington."
He begins to recite with feeling:

> "Thy ev'ry action let the Goddess guide.
> A crown, a mansion, and a throne that shine,
> With gold unfading, Washington! We thine.

"And then that glistening rust-black Stray Leechfield. We
saw him as nothing but a low-down molasses-slurper and a
mutton thief, but do you know what he did? He was stealing
chickens—methodically, not like the old days when they'd
steal one or two and try to duck the BBs. He had taken so many
over a period of time that he was over in the other county, big
as you please, dressed up like a gentleman, smoking a seegar
and driving a carriage which featured factory climate-control
air conditioning, vinyl top, AM/FM stereo radio, full leather
interior, power-lock doors, six-way power seat, power windows,
white-wall wheels, door-edge guards, bumper impact strips,
rear defroster and soft-ray glass.

"It was full of beautiful women fanning themselves and
filling the rose-tinted air with their gay laughter. He had set up
his own poultry business, was underselling everybody in eggs,
gizzards, gristles, livers—and had a reputation far and wide for
his succulent drumsticks. Had a white slave fronting for him
for ten percent. Well, when my man finally discovered him
after finding he'd built a dummy to look like him so we'd think
he was still in the fields, do you know what he did, Mr. Lincoln?
He stabbed the man. Stabbed him and fled on a white horse,
his cape furling in the wind. It was very dramatic.

"You defend Negro ruffians like that, Mr. Lincoln? You
yourself, Mr. President, said that you were never in favor of

bringing about social and political equality with them. You don't want them to vote, either. I mean, I read that in the newspaper. They're not like us, Mr. Lincoln. You said yourself that there are physical differences. Now you know you said it, Mr. Lincoln. When General Frémont got brash and freed the slaves in the Western territory, you overruled his proclamation, and now the military man tells me that you have some sort of wild proclamation on your desk you're about to sign, if this compensatory thing doesn't work."

"I haven't made up my mind yet, Mr. Swille. I guess I'm a little wishy-washy on the subject still. But . . . well, sometimes I just think that one man enslaving another man is wrong. Is wrong. Is very wrong." Lincoln pounds the table.

"Well, I won't try to influence your decision, Mr. President. Would you like Uncle Robin to help you with one of those sacks?"

"Thank you, Mr. Swille."

Uncle Robin goes over and helps Lincoln with two of the heavy gold bags.

"And before you leave, Mr. President, go down to the kitchen and have Barracuda the Mammy fix you a nice snack. She'll be so thrilled. All she talks about is Massa Lincoln, Massa Lincoln. Maybe you can sign a few autographs."

Swille rises and walks over to Lincoln, who is now standing, his hands heavy with sacks of gold. "And think before you sign that proclamation, Mr. President. The slaves like it here. Look at this childish race. Uncle Robin, don't you like it here?"

"Why, yessuh, Mr. Swille! I loves it here. Good something to eat when you wonts it. Color TV. Milk pail fulla toddy. Some whiskey and a little nookie from time to time. We gets whipped with a velvet whip, and there's free dental care and always a fiddler case your feets get restless."

"You see, Mr. President. They need someone to guide them through this world of woe or they'll hurt themselves."

"I'll certainly consider your views when I make my decision, Mr. Swille. Well, I have to go now. And thanks for contributing to the war chest, Mr. Swille."

"Sure, Lincoln, anything you say." Swille goes to the window. "Hey, I think the escort Lee sent up has arrived. Look, Lincoln, I'm throwing a little shindig for Mr. and Mrs. Jefferson Davis. Why don't you come down? I'd like to get you two together for one day. Take time off from the war."

"You can arrange that, Mr. Swille?"

"I can arrange anything. They called my father God's God, Mr. President. Davis may hate your flag and you, but everybody salutes *our* flag. Gold, energy and power: that's our flag. Now, you have to leave, Abe, and don't knock over any of the *objets d'art* in the hall. I don't think your United States Treasury [chuckle] can replace them."

"I'll be careful," Lincoln says. "I'm glad you could spend some time with me, Mr. Swille."

"Not at all, Lincoln. Have a good journey back to your yacht, and, Robin, help Mr. Lincoln with his bags of gold."

Lincoln and Swille shake hands. Lincoln and Robin begin to exit with the gold. Barracuda comes in, eying both of them suspiciously.

"Massa Swille, there's some poor-white trash down in the kitchen walking on my kitchen flo. I told them to get out my kitchen and smacked one of them on the ear with my broom."

"That's Mr. Lincoln's party, Mammy Barracuda. I want you to meet the President of the United States, Mr. Abraham Lincoln."

"Oh, Mr. Linclum! Mr. Linclum! I admires you so. Now you come on down to the kitchen and let me make you and your party a nice cup of coffee."

"But I have very important business to do on *The River Queen,* the tide of battle . . ."

"Shush your mouth and come on down here get some of this coffee. Steaming hot. What's wrong with you, man, you gone pass up some of this good old Southern hospitality?"

Lincoln shrugs his shoulders. "Well," he says, smiling, "I guess one little cup won't hurt." She waltzes around with Abe Lincoln, who follows awkwardly. She sings, "Hello, Abbbbbe. Well, hello, Abbbbbe. It's so nice to have you here where you belong."

The President blushes; he finds it hard to keep in a giggle. Swille and Robin join in, clapping their hands: "You're looking swell, Abbbeee. I can tell, Abbeeee. You're still growin', you're still goin . . ."

Barracuda and Lincoln waltz out of the room. Uncle Robin follows with the bag of gold, doing his own little step. Delighted, Swille chuckles from deep in his belly.

5

Inside the kitchen of the main house of Swille's plantation, Uncle Robin sits on a high stool reading some figures over the phone which have been scribbled on a sheet. He is, at the same time, munching some white-frosted Betty Crocker glossy cake and drinking coffee that Aunt Judy, his wife, has prepared for him. Next to his hand is a copy of *60 Families*.

"... and slave quarters number 3 wants to put 259, 344, and 544 in the box ... What you mean? Chicago, it's an hour behind in your time, it ain't too late." He hears footsteps approaching. "Hey, somebody's coming. I got to go." Uncle Robin takes a sip of coffee, looks innocent and begins to hum a spiritual. It's Moe, the white house slave.

"Uncle Robin, are you abusing your phone privileges? I don't know why the Master lets you use it. He doesn't let any of us use it."

"Oh, Mr. Moe, I was just ringing in the supplies for the week. I didn't mean no harm."

"I don't know why he trusts you, Uncle Robin. He thinks you're docile, but sometimes it seems to me that you're the cleverest of them all, though I can't prove it."

Uncle Robin stares blankly at him.

"Well, I guess you are pretty simple. I don't know what gives me the notion that you're more complex than you seem."

Moe goes to the kitchen table. Uncle Robin rises, fetches a cup of coffee and places it in front of Moe.

"What did you think of President Lincoln's visit?"

"What you say, Mr. Moe?"

"That visit. You were right there in the room."

"Oh, that. I don't understand what they be saying. I never did understand good Anglish—it takes me even an effort to read the Bible good."

"You are impoverished, aren't you? No wonder they call you an Uncle Tom."

Uncle Robin ignores this, eating another slice of cake. "I don't know, Mr. Moe, suh. Sometimes it seems to me that we are all Uncle Toms. Take yourself, for example. You are a white man but still you a slave. You may not look like a slave, and you dress better than slaves do, but all day you have to run around saying Yessuh, Mr. Swille, and Nossuh, Mr. Swille, and when Mitchell was a child, Maybe so, l'il Swille. Why, he can fire you anytime he wants for no reason."

"What! What did you say? How dare you talk to a white man like that!"

"Well, sometimes I just be reflectin, suh. Ain't no harm in that."

"Well, you can just stop your reflectin and if I hear you talkin like that again, I'm going to report to Massa Swille of your insolence, do you hear? Now you behave yourself and don't you ever let me hear you making such statements."

But before Uncle Robin can issue some apologies, saying that the devil must have gotten ahold of his tongue or that he will promise not to express such notions again, the red light above the kitchen door begins to blink, which means that Massa Swille wants Moe to come into his office. Moe wipes his mouth with a napkin, gulps the coffee down so quickly it stains his junior executive's shirt.

"Oh, dammit, now what will I do?"

"Hold on, Mr. Moe." Uncle Robin rushes to the cabinet, takes out some spot remover and dabs it on Moe's shirt. The button-down collar's stain disappears. Moe rushes out of the kitchen.

Part II
LINCOLN
THE PLAYER

6

Lincoln salutes the Confederate soldiers Lee has sent up to escort him and his party back to *The River Queen.* He climbs into the carriage and sits next to an aide.

"Did you sell him some bonds?" the aide asks.

"Yeah," Lincoln says, leaning back in his carriage, removing his stovepipe hat and boots; he takes off his white gloves last.

"Gilded Age ding-dong if there ever was. Hands like a woman's. I feel like a minstrel . . ."

"But you did sell him some bonds?"

"Yes. First I gave him the yokel-dokel—he saw through that. And then he went on about my lack of culture and poked fun at my clothes. Talked about my shiny suitcoat and pants. Then he said some nasty things about Mary. Well, I know that she's . . . she's odd. Well, you know, I couldn't stand there and listen to that, so I blew my top."

"And he still gave you the gold?"

"Yeah. You know, if we lost this war we wouldn't be able to repay Swille. We're sticking our necks out, but with the cost of things these days, we have to turn to him. Why, we still owe a bill for that Scotch plaid cap and cloak I bought so I could enter the Capitol in disguise. The Confederates thought I was

frightened, but that wasn't it at all. I was trying to duck the
bill collectors who were holding me responsible for the debts
owed by the last administration. Buchanan said there'd be days
like this. No wonder he was trembling when he shook my hand
at the inaugural ceremony, and when I was sworn in—whiz—
he took off down the platform steps. Said he had to catch a
train. Said 'Good luck, Hoosier.' Now I know what he meant."

"It was a close call, when the Confederates came up to
the house just now. You should have seen the secret service
men in the next carriage scramble from the Queen Mary. I
don't think they know what in the hell they're doing. And I
think one of them, that fat one, is a little off into the bottle.
Mr. President, you ought to fire that one."

"I don't plan to fire that one. Just put him on detail at
insignificant events. The theatre. I might need Swille's support
some more and so I'm going to start doing more for culture.
Tidy up my performance. I want you to get me and Mary Todd
some tickets to a theatre from time to time and invite Ulysses
and his wife."

"Look, sir."

On the side of the road some of the colored contraband
were appearing. They started waving their handkerchiefs at the
President. The President waved back. One man ran up to the
carriage; Lincoln stuck his hand out to shake the slave's hand,
but instead of shaking the President's hand the man began
kissing it until he dropped back behind the carriage. He stood
in the road waving.

"They love you, sir."

"Curious tribe. There's something, something very human about them, something innocent and . . . Yet I keep
having the suspicion that they have another mind. A mind kept
hidden from us. They had this old mammy up there. She began
singing and dancing me around. The first time in these years
I took my mind off the war. I felt like crawling into her lap and
going to sleep. Just sucking my thumb and rolling my hair up
into pickaninny knots. I never even gave spooks much thought,
but now that they've become a subplot in this war, I can't get

these shines off my mind. My dreams . . . She must do Swille a lot of good."

"She didn't treat us very well; told us to abandon her kitchen."

Lincoln laughs. "You know, I can't help thinking sometimes that the rich are retarded. That Swille couldn't go to the bathroom, I'll bet, without an escort or someone showing him the way. And do you know what he subsists on?"

"What, sir?"

"Slave mothers' milk."

"What?"

"It's supposed to reverse the aging process. Said he got the idea from some fellow named Tennyson. Sir Baron Lord Tennyson. Sounds like one of those fellows we used to beat up and take lunch money from back in Springfield. Anyway, Swille says he got the solution from the hormone of a reptile, and that this Tennyson fellow wrote a poem about it. One depressing work, if you'd ask my opinion. All about immortality and ennui. These people down here don't seem to do nothin but despair. This Tennyson guy was talking about flowers a lot. Do you know of him? Is he all right? And who is this ennui feller?"

"Ennui means . . . well . . . it's like a languor, a general discontent concerning the contemporary milieu. Tennyson, he's an aesthete, Mr. President."

"Well, I'll be as dull as a Kansas moon. You say he's what?"

"An aesthete. He knows about flowers, reads poetry aloud lying on French Impressionist picnic grass. Visits the lofts of painters. Attends all of the openings. Is charming and fascinating with the women."

"Well, I don't think that this Swille fellow's got all of his potatoes. He said something about a town named Camelot. Where is this town, aide? How far away is this town Camelot? Is it a train stop? Is it in Virginia?"

"Camelot is the mythical city of the Arthurian legend, Mr. Lincoln."

"Well, I'll be a flying fish on a worm tree. This Swille kept talking about the place and about how a king was going to rule America. I think he was trying to buy me off. That's my last dealings with him. His kind make you feel like . . . what's the name of the character in Mrs. Stowe's novel?"

"Uncle Tom, sir?"

"That's it. They have you tommy to them. The man started to talk strange, a lot of scimble-skamble, about knighthood and the 'days that were' . . . Hey, what the hell's going on down here, anyway? Did you hear all that screaming back there? Nobody even noticed. I didn't say nothin cause I figured if nobody noticed it, then I must be hearing things. Did you notice it, aide, all that screaming going on back there?"

Lincoln rested his head against the window and looked out into the Virginia night, the blackest night in the South. There was an old folk art cemetery with leaning tombstones behind an ornate black wrought-iron fence. A woman in white floated across the cemetery. A wolf howled. Bats flew into the dark red sun.

"Aide, did you see that?"

"I can't see anything for the fog, sir. But I think I did hear some screaming. As soon as we entered Virginia we heard the screaming. First a little screaming and then a whole lot. As soon as the sun goes up out here you hear the screaming until the moon goes down, I hear tell, Mr. Lincoln."

"Like hell."

"What's that, Mr. President?"

"The screaming, it reminds you of hell. This man Swille was talking about whips and said something about people being humiliated. Is that some kind of code?"

"Grant said it was decadent down here, Mr. Lincoln. Said it was ignoble. Others call it 'immoral.' William Wells Brown, the brown writer, called it that."

"Grant said ignoble?" Lincoln laughs. "Swille offered me a barony. What's that all about?"

"I heard talk, Mr. President. The proceedings from the Montgomery Convention where the slaveholders met to map the Confederacy have never been released, but there are ru-

mors that somebody offered Napoleon III the Confederate
Crown, and he said he'd think about it. It was in *The New York
Times*, August—"

"The Crown!"

"But Nappy Three said that slavery was an anachronism."

"Hey!" Lincoln said, snapping his fingers. "I got it! Of
course."

"What's that, Mr. President?"

"Look, it's common sense. Why, I'll be a jitterbug in a
hogcreek. Aide, when we return to Washington, I want you to
return Swille's gold. We don't need it."

"But, Mr. President, we just risked our lives coming
through Confederate lines to get the gold. Now you don't want
it? I don't understand."

"We change the issues, don't you see? Instead of making
this some kind of oratorical minuet about States' Rights versus
the Union, what we do is make it so that you can't be for the
South without being for slavery! I want you to get that portrait
painter feller Denis Carter to come into the office, where he'll
show me signing the . . . the Emancipation Proclamation.
That's it. The Emancipation Proclamation. Call in the press.
Get the Capitol calligrapher who's good at letterin to come in
and draw this Proclamation. Phone the networks. We'll put an
end to this Fairy Kingdom nonsense. Guenevere, Lancelot,
Arthur and the whole dang-blasted genteel crew."

"A brilliant idea, Mr. President. A brilliant idea."

"And I want you to clear the White House of those office
seekers and others pestering me all day. Wanting to shake my
hand. Do you know what some bird asked me the other day?"

"What, Mr. President?"

"The jackass called me long-distance collect when the
rates are at their peak and wanted me to do something about
a cow he'd bought that had been pumped full of water so's to
make it look like the critter weighed more than it did. Well,
I called the fellow he bought it from and the fellow said that
if the farmer produced a bill of sale he'd return the money.
Well, I called the farmer and told him what the other fellow

said and then the farmer said he couldn't find the bill of sale and wanted me to take the first train out of Washington to help him look for it. Said he needed someone to watch the cow, who was some high-strung critter. Well, I don't think we can tie up the federal machinery on business like that, aide. And another thing, Swille seems to know more about the government's business than I do. I want you to investigate the leaks. Did you send Major Corbett away?"

"We put Major Corbett on active duty, Mr. President."

"Good. Invite Mrs. Corbett to review the troops with me and General Hooker tomorrow. Tell her afterwards we'll take tea. Give my boots a little lick of grease and go to the drugstore and get me some of that Golden Fluid hair slick."

"But what will I do about Mrs. Lincoln, Mr. President? The press will be there. Suppose they take a picture?"

"Oh, tell Mother . . . tell her that I was detained. I don't know which one's going to be the death of me, Mother or the niggers."

"How much gold did Mr. Swille give you, Mr. President?"

Lincoln counts. "He was supposed to give me five, but I only count four."

"What could have happened, sir? The nigger?"

"I doubt it. Poor submissive creature. You should have seen him shuffle about the place. Yessirring and nosirring. Maybe he didn't intend to give me but four. I'm tired. Can't you make this thing go faster?"

"Yessir," the aide says. "Right away, sir."

He leans out of the window and instructs the coachman to go faster. Lincoln opens his purse and examines the five-dollar Confederate bill. Bookie odds favored the Union, but you could never tell when you might need carfare.

7

Cato the Graffado overseer, sandy hair, freckles, "aquiline" nose, rushes into Arthur Swille's office.

"Massa Swille! Massa Swille!"

"What is it, you infernal idiot," says Swille, scolding the man who bears a remarkable resemblance to himself, in fact, could be a butterscotched version of him. Cato is trembling, his silver platform shoes fixed to the floor, the carnation in his lapel twitching.

"Now what do you want? Speak up. I don't have all day."

"Massa Swille, I found out where them sables is hidin. 40s and them."

"You what?" Swille says, now on his feet, staring at the man.

"Them sables, they hidin around the great lakes."

"Good work, boy. How did you find out?"

"This girl I went to General Howard's Civilizing School with. She . . . she got a job at *Beulahland Review,* and they gettin ready to publish his poem 'Flight to Canada.' In the poem he refers to our women in a most anti-suffragette manner. She said she smuggled it out and let some of her friends in the New York Suffragette Society read it, and she say they told her to burn it. They have meetings on Fourteenth Street in New York, she say . . ."

"Would you cut the trivial details and tell me where those rascals are?"

"Emancipation City. She say that she was fixin to play like it never came in and when he called up there asking about it, she told him that all the editors were in conference, or that they'd gone for the day. She was too late, Massa Swille, because the mens hab already writ the rascal that it's comin out in a forthcoming issue. There's nothing she can do about it now."

"Which kink wrote it, Cato?"

"Raven Quickskill. The poem say that he has come back here to the plantation a lots and that he has drunk up all your wine and that he tricked your wife into giving him the combination to your safe. And he say he poisoned your Old Crow. And to add to the worser, Massa Swille, he say somethin cryptic. Somethin about . . . Well, I don't precisely understand, Massa Swille, but he say somethin about your favorite quadroon giving him some . . . some 'She-Bear.' What on earth do that mean, Massa Swille?"

"Skip it, Cato. Nothing your puerile Christian ears would be interested in."

"Oh, thank you, Massa Swille. Thank you, Massa Swille. The part about Canada is just done to throw you off his trail. That nigger ain't in no Canada. There ain't no such place; that's just reactionary mysticism. I never seed no Canada, so there can't be none. The only thing exists is what I see. Seeing is believing."

"Call out my tracers, my claimants, my nigger catchers and my bloodhounds. Arm my paddyrollers. Call Maryland!"

Cato begins to run around the room, until he bumps into a bust of Caligula, Swille's favorite hero of antiquity, and knocks it to the floor.

"Look what you did, you idiot. Busted one of my *objets d'art.* Never mind. Do you have a copy of the poem?"

"That I do, suh. That I do. I was clever enough to have a Xerox made. And if you ask me, it don't have no redeeming qualities, it is bereft of any sort of *pièce de résistance,* is cute and unexpurgated . . ."

"Spare me the cotton stuffing, Cato. No one's interested in your critical abilities and you know what they did in the old days to the messenger who brought bad news."

"But, Mr. Swille, you sent me to school for that. To be critical about things. They gibbed me a Ph.D. Don't you remember?"

"I do, Cato. [Calmer] I hear the slaves calling you names, vilifying you. Don't pay any attention. Jump over the broom with any of the tar wenches you see."

"Yes, sir! Thank you, sir! Thank you also for giving me such a good education. I knows the Bible by heart. I knows things like 'standards,' and how to pronounce 'prolegomenon.' I caught some of them praying to them old filthy fetishes the other day; they seemed to be habbin a good time too. I called in the overseer, and he give them a good flogging. That he did. Whipped them darkies. And last week I told them slaves: no more polygamy. This savage custom they brought from Tarzan country. They's allowed only one woman, suh. I told the women anyone they see with another woman they can shoot. I armed the women slaves. They'll keep order. They'll dismember them niggers with horrifying detail."

"So you've just about ended this heathenism, eh, Cato? Their ethnicity."

"That I've done, suh. It was mighty helpful of you and Barracuda to end all them cults and superstitions and require that all the people follow only the Jesus cult. That make them work harder for you, Boss. The women especially be thrilled with the Jesus cult. They don't ask no questions any more. They's accepted their lot. Them other cults, Massa . . . there was too many of them. Horn cults, animal cults, ghost cults, tree cults, staff cults, serpent cults—everything they see they make a spurious cult out of it. Some of them kinks is worshipping the train, boss. They know the time when each train pass by on the railroad tracks. Leechfield even had a cassarette, Massa Swille."

"A what?"

"One of them things you talk into, and your voice come

back. Boss, even with my liberal education, it looked like magic. I was skeered. But I didn't show it."

"Oh, you mean a cassette."

"That's the one; it sure is the one, Massa Swille. The nigger was having runners going from village to village carrying messages refutin me and my Biblical arguments. I found them cassarettes and throwed them into the river, Massa. He was just confusin everybody. I'm glad that old Leechfield is gone."

"Good, son. I mean—"

They freeze and stare at each other.

"Oh, figuratively, Cato. Only figuratively. I call all my sbleezers son. Now, Cato, I'm giving you new responsibilities. First, I want you to send in the Nebraska Tracers. Try to reason with them. Honey them with saccharin and seduce them through flowery, intelligent proposals."

"Yessir, Massa Swille. Yessir. It sound like an exciting prospect."

"And if they don't go for that, I want you to permit the bloodhounds to sniff Xerox copies of that poem. The way you find a fugitive, remember, is to go all the way back and work your way up to him. That poem has trapped him once and it'll trap him again. Now you go to it, Cato."

"Yessir."

"Hustle, Cato, hustle."

"Yessir." His arms thrown out in front, his heels kicking his behind, Cato rushes out of the door and knocks over Uncle Robin, who's been listening through the keyhole; the glasses of Scotch he has placed on the tray tumble to the floor, spilling on Cato's white shoes. Cato's monocle drops to his chest. "Now look what you did, old splay-nosed rascal," he says angrily.

"I'm sorry, Mister Cato, but I thought maybe you and Massa Swille would like some 'freshments."

" 'Freshments, 'freshments. When are you going to learn? Refreshments. How are we goin to gain acceptance if we don't show that we know Dr. Johnson and them."

"There's some spot remover in the kitchen, Mr. Cato."

"Oh, all right. And don't get smart, either, just because Harriet Beecher Stowe came down and taped you. Ha! Ha! She didn't even use your interview. Used Tom over at the Legree plantation. What did she give you?"

"She just gave me a flat-out fee. I bought a pig, a dog and a goose with it."

"Ha! Ha! Eeeee. Ha! Ha!" Cato stands in the hall and slaps his head. "One of the best sellers of all time and you only received pig money. You are stupid, just like they say, you black infidel."

"Yessir, Mr. Cato."

Cato, whistling, skips down the hall toward the kitchen. Uncle Robin stares after him. A stare that could draw out the dust in a brick.

8

About a mile from the Great Castle are the Frederick Douglass Houses. This is where all the Uncles and Aunties who work in the Great Castle live. Inside a penthouse, in one of the bedrooms, Uncle Robin and Aunt Judy lie under the covers of a giant waterbed, watching TV. It is twelve o'clock midnight. Their children, whose freedom they've bought with their toil, are "Free Negroes" who live in New York. They send their parents money and write them letters about the good life up North. Robin and Judy know about the North from the conversations they've heard at the Swille table from visitors. They know that the arriving immigrants are molesting the Free Negroes in the Northern cities. They know that Harriet Beecher Stowe characterized the worst slave traders as being Vermonters. They know a thing or two and are proud of their children. Even though their children chastise them about their "old ways" and call them Uncles and Aunts and refer to themselves as 1900's people. There is a bottle of champagne on the dresser. Robin and Judy are sipping from glasses. A panel of newsmen is discussing the Emancipation of the slaves.

Uncle Robin sighs. "Well, I guess Lincoln went on and crossed Swille. Swille was downstairs calling Texas when I got off duty a half-hour ago. I knew that Lincoln was a player. Man, he was outmaneuvering Swille like a snake. Me and him winked at each other from time to time. Ugliest man you want to see. Look like Alley Oop. When Swille brought out the Old Crow, Lincoln's eyes lit up. You suppose it's true what that Southern lady said about Lincoln being in the White House drunk for six hours at a time? I understand that Grant is a lush, too; what's wrong with these white people?"

Aunt Judy's thigh rubbed against his. Their shoulders touched. She took a sip of champagne. "You should see Ms. Swille. She drinks like a fish. Won't eat. Look like a broomstick. I went into the room the other day and look like Mammy Barracuda had a half nelson on the woman. They stopped doing whatever they were doing, and I played like nothing was unusual. Then, later on in the day, Barracuda came into the kitchen, and we turned off the radio because we were listening to Mr. Lincoln's address, but she caught us. She asked us did we know what Emancipation meant, and we sort of giggled and she did too. Then Barracuda showed us the Bible where it say 'He that knoweth his master's will and doeth it not, shall be beaten with many stripes.' "

"I never read it, but I figured something like that was in it."

"She said that we were property and that we should give no thoughts to running away. She say she'd heard that 40s, Quickskill and Leechfield were having a hard time of it and that Quickskill had gone crazy and was imagining that he was in Canada. She said that she always knew Quickskill was crazy. As for Canada, she said they skin niggers up there and makes lampshades and soap dishes out of them, and it's more barbarous in Toronto than darkest Africa, a place where we come from and for that reason should pray hard every night for the Godliness of a man like Swille to deliver us from such a place."

"What's wrong with that woman? Seem like the older she get, the sillier she get. In the old times people used to get wiser the older they get. Now it's all backwards. Everything is backwards."

"She treats that Bangalang like a dog. Whips her. Today

for dropping a cake. Sure is a lot of whipping going on up there. They whips people when they ain't even done nothing. They had a party the other night—the gentlemen from the Magnolia Baths, and they was whipping on each other too."

"It's the war, Judy. Making everybody nervous. As soon as old man Swille heard about the Emancipation you should've seen him. That cigar bout jumped out his face. He started cussing and stamping his foot. He called Washington, but they gave him the runaround. The boys in the telegraph office called him Arthur and made indignant proposals to him, so he say. Them Yankees are a mess. Well, the Planters have been driving up to the Castle all day now. Those Planters are up to no good."

The bottom of her foot moved across the top of one of his. The top of his right thigh was resting on her hip. He was talking low, in her ear.

"Rub my neck a little, hon."

He began to rub her neck.

She sighed. "That's nice."

"Did you hear what the runner up from Mississippi said?"

"What, Robin?"

"Say he saw Quickskill's picture in the newspaper way down there."

"Was it a personal runaway ad that old man Swille put in there?"

"No, it was something about a poem of his."

"Oh, that must have been the poem I heard Cato discussing with Swille. All about him coming back here. I didn't see him come back. Did you hear anything from the fields?"

"Nobody seen him here."

"Say Ms. Swille showed him the combination to her safe."

"That Quickskill. Boy, he was something."

They both laugh.

"Remember that time, Judy, when he complained to Massa Swille that Mammy Barracuda would always serve his dinner cold and put leftovers in his meal?"

"Sometimes she wouldn't even put silverware out for Raven."

"She didn't like it because he was Swille's private secretary and sat at the table with the family."

"She didn't like anyone to come between her and Arthur, as she calls him."

Aunt Judy turns to him and puts her arms around his neck, their abdomens, thighs, touching, her cheek brushing against his as she places the champagne glass on the table next to the bed.

"Want some more?"

"I'll be drunk, Robin. I have to get up tomorrow at six and get breakfast."

"One more. For the Emancipation."

"Won't do us any good. He freed the slaves in the regions of the country he doesn't have control over, and in those he does have control over, the slaves are still slaves. I'll never understand politics."

Robin is sitting up, the covers down to his naked waist. He picks up the champagne bottle and pours.

"That's Lincoln playing. Lincoln is a player. The Emperor of France's secretary called up here and told Swille not to show up to that party for the royal people next week. Swille tried to get through to the Emperor, but the secretary refused, and when Swille called the Emperor by his first name, the secretary said to Swille, 'Don't you slave peddler ever be calling him that again,' and hung up, in French." They laugh. "Is Ms. Swille still on her strike?"

"Is she! Today she called me and Bangalang her sisters and said something about all of us being in the same predicament. Me and Bangalang just looked at each other."

"She used to be so beautiful."

"Wasn't she so! The belle of the Charity Ball. Horse rider. Miss Mississippi for 1850, same time Arthur got his award."

"When do you think they're going to tell her about her son?"

"You mean how he got eat—Oh, that reminds me. I mean to tell you. Speaking of the dead. Well, Bangalang told us today that one of the children was out in the cemetery and they wandered into the crypt where that old hateful Vivian, Arthur's sister, is, and that the child saw . . ."

"What . . . what she see?"

"As she said, she heard somebody talking and he went inside, and the child saw Massa Swille and the man had done taken off the lid from the crypt and was on top of his sister and was crying and sobbing, and that he was sweating and that he was making so much noise that he didn't even notice the child and the child run away, and the child say he saw Vivian's decomposed hand clinging to his neck."

"That kid's got to be telling a fib, Judy. I told you about letting those children play in the cemetery."

"But, Robin, ain't nothin in there but dead folks."

A low moan of a solitary wolf can be heard.

"Oh, there go that wolf again. I hope he's not out there all night again. Judy . . . Judy?"

Robin turns over and sees that his wife is asleep. They are back to back.

9

Raven Quickskill was sitting in a house with black shutters on Free Street in Emancipation City. It is an eighteenth-century schoolhouse he is "watching" for a few months. The owners, Sympathizers to the Cause, had left for a resort in another state, and knowing that he was a "fuge," as a person of his predicament was called, had asked him to watch it. That's the way it was in the fugitive life. Minding things for Abolitionists and Sympathizers to the Cause. They had left some plants, which he tended. And some cats. He was sitting in a rocker, reading a book about Canada, about the plentiful supply of gasoline, the cheap, clean hotel rooms that could be had in Toronto and Montreal; the colorful Eskimo sculpture that could be bought in the marketplace; the restaurants specializing in lobster; the scuba diving, the deep-sea fishing.

There was a knock at the door. He opened it on two men. They were dressed in blazers and wore grey slacks, black cordovans. They were very neat. One was medium-sized, the other, squat, short. The short one was carrying a briefcase.

"Mr. Quickskill?" the man with the briefcase asked.

"That's me."

"We have orders to repossess you," said the medium-sized one. He sneezed. Removed a handkerchief and blew his nose.

Quickskill was thinking. It was three years since they had sent him a bill. He'd been moving ever since. They'd found him.

"Here's my card," the medium-sized man said, sneezing again.

"Have a cold?" Quickskill asked, reading the card. The card said NEBRASKA TRACERS, INC. "I have some vitamin C in the cabinet."

"Hey, Harold," the man with the briefcase said, "that might help. Vitamin C."

"Would you gentlemen come in," Quickskill said, escorting them into the room of Shaker furniture. They walked across the waxed hardwood floors and sat down. "Can I offer you something?" he asked, cool.

"No," they said.

Quickskill clasped his hands on a knee, lifting his feet off the floor a bit. "Now, you gentlemen said that you were going to repossess me."

"Your lease on yourself has come to an end. You are overdue. According to our information, Mr. Swille owns you," the short one said, reaching into his briefcase. "Here's the bill of sale. You see, Mr. Swille sees you as a bargain. Bookkeeper, lecturer, an investment that paid off. He's anxious to get you back, and since there are a lot of invoices and new shipments piling up, he says a man of your ability is indispensable."

"Uncle Robin is performing that function now. He needs Uncle Robin in the house. Robin's overextending himself," the medium one said. "He's reading and writing now. Seems to have begun to assess his condition. One of the white house slaves, Moe, reported that the old codger had taken to philosophizing. Swille says he's concluded that the missing invoices and forged papers will be ignored. He blames the whole thing on your misled humanitarian impulses."

"And if I don't want to return to Virginia, then what?"

"We'll have no choice but to foreclose," the short one said.

"Look," the medium one said, "I hate doing this but . . . but it's the law."

"Even Mr. Lincoln said that what a man does with his property is his own affair," said the short one.

"Yeah, Lincoln," murmured Quickskill.

"What?"

"Oh, nothing."

"You're lucky, if you ask me. Why, that poem you wrote . . ." the short one said.

"How did you know?" It had been nearly three winters since *Beulahland Review* promised to publish it. Maybe Swille owned *Beulahland* too.

"Mr. Swille gave us a copy. You know, if we weren't his employees, we'd circulate it ourselves," the short one said.

"Regardless of the copyright?" the medium one asked.

"Oh, I forgot. That's the law. We must obey the law, though he doesn't come within the framework of Anglo-Saxon law. Justice Taney said that a slave has no rights that a white man is bound to respect."

"Is it autobiographical?" the medium one asked Quickskill.

"I'm afraid it isn't," Quickskill answered.

"See, I told you. They have poetic abilities, just like us. They're not literal-minded, as Mr. Jefferson said. I knew that he couldn't have possibly managed all of those things. Sneak back to the plantation three or four times. Know about poisons," the medium one said. "That would have been too complicated for a slave."

"You see, Mr. Swille, we're students at a progressive school in Nebraska. We're just doing this job to pay for tuition in graduate school. We've even read your poetry," said the short one.

"You have?"

"Yes. *The Anthology of Ten Slaves,* they had it in the anthropology section of the library," the medium one said.

"I'm a Whitman man, myself," the short one said.

"Really?" Quickskill said. "Isn't it strange? Whitman desires to fuse with Nature, and here I am, involuntarily, the comrade of the inanimate, but not by choice."

"I don't understand," they said together.

"I am property. I am a thing. I am in the same species as any other kind of property. We form a class, a family of things. This long black deacon's bench decorated with painted white roses I'm sitting on is worth more than me—five hundred dollars. Superior to me."

"Fine thought. Fine thought. You see, I told you they can think in the abstract," the short one said.

They were looking at the painting on the wall. Abraham Lincoln, armed with a gun swab, fighting the dragon of rebellion who has the face of a pig. A short pipe-smoking man has chained Abe's leg to the tree of "constitutionality" and "democracy." Lincoln became dictator after Fort Sumter. Told Congress not to return to Washington until the Fourth of July.

"Excuse me, I forgot the vitamin C," Quickskill said.

"Of course," the short one said. "Thanks for remembering."

They picked up a copy of a first edition of Harriet Beecher Stowe's *Uncle Tom's Cabin.* As Quickskill walked into the bathroom, he heard the short one say, "I hear she made a pile on this book."

Quickskill, the property, moved past the bowl, the sink, and to the window. He opened it quietly. He climbed out and jumped, landing on the ground of an alley. He went by the open window, ducking. The men could be seen talking. He started to run. It was easy for him to run, and he was fast. He had burned the fat from his waist running through the streets of Emancipation City. Nebraskaites. Nice, clean-cut killers. Human being-burglars. Manhandlers. Always putting the sack on things. Putting anacondas in the Amazon in a sack. Trapping a jaguar with dogs, then lassoing the jaguar from above, lifting the jaguar, then lowering the jaguar into a net. Sacking things. Jump on the armadillo from a horse and sack the armadillo. Well, they aren't going to sack me, Quickskill thought. Nebraskaites. Now he understood Elymas Payson Rogers' poem:

> But all the blind Nebraskaites
> Who have invaded human rights,

Will at the North in every case
Be overwhelmed in deep disgrace.
When their eventful life is o'er,
No one their loss will much deplore;
And when their kindred call their name,
Their cheeks will mantle o'er with shame;
But soon their names will be forgot,
The memory of them all shall rot.
And let their burying places be
Upon the coast beside the sea;
And let the ever-rolling surge
Perform a constant funeral dirge.
And when the stranger shall demand
Why these are buried in the sand,
Let him be told without disguise:
They trod upon the Compromise.

10

The Slave Hole Café is where the "community" in Emancipation City hangs out. The wallpaper shows a map of the heavens. Prominent is the North Star. A slave with rucksack is pointing it out to his dog. The café is furnished with tables, chairs, sofas, from different periods. There are quite a few captain's chairs, deacon's benches. There are posters and paintings and framed programs: *Our American Cousin,* a play by Tom Tyler; a photo of Lincoln boarding a train on the way back to Washington from a trip to Emancipation. Sawdust on the floor. A barrel of dill pickles. Above the long bar is a sign: PABST BLUE RIBBON. Corn-row and nappy-haired field slaves are here as well as a quadroon or two. Carpetbaggers, Abolitionists, Secessionists, or "Seceshes," as they are called, even some Copperheads. The secret society known as the "Rattlesnake" order meets here. They advertise their meetings in the Emancipation newspaper: "Attention, Rattlesnakes, come out of your holes . . . by order of President Grand Rattle. Poison Fang, Secretary."

Confederate sympathizers go to places named the Alabama Club, but some come here, too. They've been known to smash a bottle after a slave has drunk from it. Ducktail hairdos go here. Crossbars of the Confederate fly from pickup trucks.

Quickskill ran into the Slave Hole out of breath, went to a table where he saw Leechfield's Indentured Servant friend, the Immigrant, Mel Leer. Well, he wasn't indentured any more. He had served his contract and was now at liberty. He and Leechfield were inseparable. When he plopped into the chair the Immigrant rustled his newspaper in annoyance. His hair was wild, uncombed black curls, and he kept brushing some away from the left side of his forehead. He had an intense look, like Yul Brynner, wore long flowing ties and velvet suits and some kind of European shoes. Lace cuffs. Jewelry.

"Man, two guys just tried to confiscate me. Put a claim check on me just like I was somebody's will-call or something," panted Quickskill.

"Kvetch! Always kvetch!"

"What do you mean kvetch? If I hadn't run away, I'd be in a van on the way back to Virginia."

The waitress brought him a frosty mug of beer like the kind they feature at Sam's Chinese restaurant on Yonge Street in Toronto.

The Immigrant looked at him. "Your people think that you corner the market on the business of atrocity. My relatives were dragged through the streets of St. Petersburg, weren't permitted to go to school in Moscow, were pogrommed in Poland. There were taxes on our synagogues and even on our meat. We were forbidden to trade on Sundays and weren't allowed to participate in agriculture. They forced us into baptism against our wishes. Hooligans were allowed to attack us with weapons, and the police just stood there, laughing. Your people haven't suffered that much. I can prove it, statistically."

"Oh yeah? Nobody's stoning you in the streets here. You are doing quite well, hanging in cafés, going to parties with Leechfield. And you have a nice place to live. What are you bitchin about? All you and Leechfield seem to do is party and eat ice cream topped with crème de menthe."

"There are more types of slavery than merely material slavery. There's a cultural slavery. I have to wait as long as two weeks sometimes before I can get a *Review of Books* from New

York. This America, it has no salvation. Did you see what happened in those battles? At Bull Run? They were like picnics attended by the rich. Cowboyland. Look at this filth . . ." It was a copy of *Life* magazine; a photo of the carnage at Gettysburg. "Filth! Obscene! Disgusting! Just as this country is. Why, during the whole time I've been in this town, I haven't seen one person reading Dostoevsky. Your people! Requesting wages and leaving their plantations. They should pay for themselves. Look at us. We were responsible. We paid for ourselves. Paid our way. I earned myself! We never sassed the master, and when we were punished we always admitted that we were in the wrong. The whole world, sometimes, seems to be against us. Always passing resolutions against us. Hissing us. Nobody has suffered as much as we have."

"Nobody has suffered as much as my people," says Quickskill calmly.

The Immigrant, Mel Leer, rises. "Don't tell me that lie."

The whole café turns to the scene.

"Our people have suffered the most."

"My people!"

"My people!"

"My people!"

"My people!"

"We suffered under the hateful Czar Nicholas!"

"We suffered under Swille and Legree, the most notorious Masters in the annals of slavery!"

"Hey, what's the matter with you two?" It was Leechfield. On his arm was a Beecherite who had just come over from Boston. She looked like a human bird, her nose was so long, and she wore old-maid glasses. Her hat was covered with flowers.

"What took you so long? You were supposed to be here an hour ago," the Immigrant said, sitting down again, looking at his watch. Leechfield just stared at him with those narrow eyes. That squint. And that smile which got him into the homes and near the fire of many a female Sympathizer about town. His arm dangled over the chair in which he'd plopped down. He snapped his finger for a waitress. The cold Beecher-ite just sat there, looking at him adoringly. The waitress came.

"Gimme a Southern Comfort."

The girl giggled. Quickskill, now relaxed, even smiled. But the Immigrant, Mel Leer, looked at him, frowning.

"Look, Leer," Leechfield finally said, "I'm the one who's bringing the money into this operation."

"Yes, but you don't understand. It's more complicated than that. I was the one who introduced you to the game. I taught you the techniques of survival, when you were merely interested in getting by. You see these fingers?" Mel Leer revealed his long, lean fingers. "They've rolled dice at Monte Carlo, distilled vodka in a vodka plant, sewn furs, deftly over-whelmed superior forces while you were humming 'Old Black Joe,' you . . . you . . ."

"Hold it, man. Don't get excited. Now sit down." Meekly, Leer sat down. (What was going on here? What was this strange bond between them? A white bondsman and a black bondsman in cahoots in some enterprise.) "She ready, you ready, so let's go."

The three rose to leave. Mel Leer put the foreign-lan-guage newspaper under his arm.

"Look, Leechfield, I have to talk to you, it's important," Quickskill said.

"Can't do it now, man. Got to go. Come over to the loft sometime."

"But . . ."

The three had moved out of the café. Quickskill ordered another mug. Canada Dry this time. That morning he had heard that Air Canada was cutting its rates by thirty-five per-cent.

Everybody had turned their attention toward Canada. Barbara Walters had just about come out on national television to say that the Prime Minister of Canada, this eagle-faced man, this affable and dapper gentleman who still carried a handker-chief in the left suit pocket, was the most enlightened man in the Western world. The world expected great things from this man. His wife was a former flower child: intelligent, well-bred, capable of discussing cultural subjects on television. So good-looking!

Harry Reasoner agreed with Ms. Walters, saying that though some of his critics disapproved of the way the Prime Minister still followed the custom of attending the Potlatch, that great festival of giveaway practiced by his people, during his administration the ban on the Potlatch had been lifted. Mr. Reasoner said that this would make it possible for the Potlatch to be brought into the United States as a way of relieving the people of the dreary, sad life caused by the conflict.

Ah! Canada! There had just been a free election in Canada. The Liberal party had won 141 seats in the House of Commons. There was a picture in *Time* of the Prime Minister standing next to his wife, she holding his hand, he looking down as though his sharp Indian nose would bump her forehead. There was a big sign over the archway where they stood, written in Halloween letters: CONGRATULATIONS.

His wife said of him: "He's a beautiful guy, a very loving human being who has taught me a lot about loving."

11

Quickskill went over to the address that Stray Leechfield had given him. It was located in the old warehouse district of Emancipation City. He looked at the directory. "Leechfield & Leer." Their office was located on the third floor. He got off the elevator and walked down the hall. The door was ajar, so he walked in. He heard some people talking. One man seemed to be giving directions, telling people to move into certain positions. What was going on? He walked into the hall from the outer office and came upon an area closed off by some curtains. He opened the curtains and took a peek.

Oh my God! My God! My God! Leechfield was lying naked, his rust-colored body must have been greased, because it was glistening, and there was . . . there was—the naked New England girl was twisted about him, she had nothing on but those glasses and the flower hat. How did they manage? And then there was this huge bloodhound. He was licking, he was . . . The Immigrant was underneath one of those Brady boxes —it was flashing. He . . . he was taking daguerreotypes, or "chemical pictures."

"Hey, what's the matter with you? The sun, there's too much light. Quickskill, what's wrong with you?"

Leechfield said, "Damn." The unclothed girl looked up.

She had a strange smile on her face. Her eyes were glassy. She was panting heavily.

"I want to talk to Leechfield. It's important."

"I have to deliver this film to a distributor tonight. Make it quick," Leer told Leechfield.

"Wait outside," Leechfield said, annoyed.

Quickskill went outside. Soon Leechfield came through the curtains. He was dressed in a robe he was tying around the waist.

"What was that?" asked Quickskill.

"None of your goddam business, Quickskill. Look, man, don't you worry about me. We supposed to be free, aren't we?"

"That's true."

"Then don't handcuff yourself to me."

"What do you mean?"

"It's my bi'ness what I do. I ain't your slave, so don't be looking at me with those disapproving eyes and axing me questions."

"I . . ."

"Shit, everybody can't do anti-slavery lectures. I can't. I have to make it the best I can, man. I don't see no difference between what I'm doing and what you're doing."

"What do you mean?"

"You have to get evil-smelling eggs thrown at you, and I heard up in Buffalo they were gettin ready to throw some flour on William Wells Brown. Remember when those mobocrats beat up Douglass? Even Douglass, knocked on the ground like any old vagrant."

"I don't want to go into it. I was just shocked because I didn't expect it."

"You shocked? What you shocked about? I'm not watching no houses for nobody. I'm not feedin nobody's cats and forwarding nobody's mail. I get it this way. I pull in more in a day than you do in a whole year. You green, man. Brilliant but green. You one green Negro."

"Listen, Leechfield, I didn't come in here to get in an argument—"

"House nigger. Yes ma'am, no ma'am—you and that Uncle Robin. I see you coming down to the field village, putting on airs and shit. I used to watch you."

"If it wasn't for us, they would have discovered your game a long time before."

"What?"

"They knew about the poultry. They asked us about it when we made inventory of the eggs. We told them it was a mistake the Texas calculator made. We knew it was you. I saw you over in the other county when I was doing errands for the Swille family."

"What? And you didn't say nothin?"

"We covered for you all the time—made excuses for you and sometimes did the work ourselves that you were supposed to do. And when some of you ran away, we provided you with a map, and so some of us are traveling all over the country pleading for the Cause. So what if we get eggs thrown at us and are beaten unconscious? Swille was the one who stirred up rivalry among us. Don't you think I knew that when Swille was flattering your kind, he was making fun of us. Look, Leechfield, the reason I came up here is because, well, Swille is on our trail. Today I was visited by a couple of Nebraskaites."

"So what you bothering me for?"

"Don't you think we all ought to try to stop them?"

"Look, man"—he pulled out a wad of bills—"I sent the money to Swille. I bought myself with the money with which I sell myself. If anybody is going to buy and sell me, it's going to be me."

"That doesn't make any difference to him. I don't think he really wants us to pay for ourselves. I think he wants *us*. He thinks by sending the Tracers after us we'll be dumb enough to return, voluntarily; he thinks that a couple of white faces with papers will scare us. Why should I have to tell you all of this? You of all people. You were their hero. They egged you on when you took your stolen hens, went into business. At that time they didn't want us Mints anywhere near the business. You worked one right under their eyes. Man, Stray, you were our greased lightning, our telegraph wire, our wing-heeled Legba, warning the woodsmen and the rootmen about Barracuda and Cato's plan to replace all of the cults with one. You were the last warrior against the Jesus cult. And when they caught up with you, how extravagant your departure was. How glorious. And now, here you are with this Leer; I don't trust Russians. How can you—"

"Aw, man, Mel's all right. Look, I just want to be left alone. I'm not no hero, I just have bravado." That's what Mel said: Bravado, striking a flamboyant pose. "See, Quickskill, the difference between you and me is that you sneak, while I don't. You were the first one to hat, but you did it in a sneaky way. What kind of way was that, we thought. Just like a house slave. Tipping away. Following a white man and his wife onto the boat with a trunk on your shoulder, and when the guard ax you where you going, you say you with them. You house slaves were always tipping around, holding your shoes in your hands, trying not to disturb anybody. Well, Leer has done more for me than any of you niggers. Any of you. Always rooting for somebody, and when you do it, say we did it. I got tired of doing it. 'We did it' wasn't paying my rent. 'We did it' wasn't buying my corn, molasses and biscuits. Where was 'we did it' when I was doing without, huh? When I was broke and hungry. So I decided to do something that only I could do, so that's why I'm doing what I'm doing. What I'm doing is something 'we did it' can't do, unless we did it one at a time. You follow? Besides, I sent Swille a check. Look, Quickskill, money is what makes them go. Economics. He's got the money he paid for me, and so that satisfy him. Economics."

"Hey, Leechfield, we have some more shooting to do," Leer says, peeking through the door.

"Look, man, if you want to buy yourself, here's the money. You can pay me back."

"But it's not that simple, Leechfield. We're not property. Why should we pay for ourselves? We were kidnapped."

"Yeah, you may think so. But this is a white man's country. It never occurred to you because you thought that since you were working in the Castle . . ." He started to return to the room; he was combing his hair. "Hey, look, Quickskill, come by the pad sometime. Don't stay away." He closed the door on Quickskill.

12

Quickskill walked the streets. He kept seeing license plates with VIRGINIA on them; they seemed to be following him. He put his collar up around his neck. He put his hands in his pocket. He kept walking against the shop windows, sliding around the corners. He was a fugitive. He was what you'd call a spare fugitive instead of a busy fugitive: he didn't have the hundreds of wigs, the make-up, the quick changes busy fugitives had to go through; he was a fugitive, but there was no way he could disguise himself.

That's it, he thought, snapping his fingers—40s would know what to do. 40s lived in a houseboat down near the river.

When he climbed onto the old rusty houseboat, it was dark. He went to the door and knocked.

"Who's there?"

40s opened the door on Quickskill. He had a shotgun aimed at him.

"Aw, 40s, put it away. We're not in Virginia no more."

40s spat. "That's what you think. Shit. Virginia everywhere. Virginia outside. You might be Virginia."

All the same he put the shotgun down and took Quickskill inside. "You ought to get your own home instead of watching them for peoples. I got my home. Nothing like having your own home. Don't have to take care nobody's plants and they cats or forward they mail."

"How can a 'fuge' have his own home, 40s? Why, I'd be a sitting duck. Swille's claimants and catchers could find me any time they wished."

"I got something for them. This rifle. You and Leechfield have nothing but dreams. Your Canada. His 'show business.' You writing poems. Leechfield with that Jew . . ."

"Listen, I'll have none of that."

"He is, though. He is a Jew. He call me a Mint, why come I can't call him a Jew? He call me a Mint, don't he?"

"But—"

"Don't he! He call me a Mint, and a black man suppose that's what I don't want to call myself. Huh! Suppose I don't."

"You sound like a Nativist."

"The Nativists got good ideas. So do the Know-Nothings. I'd join them if they let me. Matter fact, let me show you."

He pulled out a hand-spun crude-looking medallion. It was mixed up with symbols that couldn't possibly go together. Strange letters. What ragged band of Bedlamites could this be? "The Order of the Star-Spangled Banner." The "S" was backwards and the "Spangled" spelled with an extra "g."

"They right. Immigrants comin over here. Raggedy Micks, Dagos and things. Jews. The Pope is behind it. The Pope finance Ellis Island. That's why it's an island. Have you ever noticed the Catholic thing about islands? The Pope and them be in them places plottin. They gettin ready to kill Lincoln so's they can rule America."

With this he pulled out some filthy saddle-stitched rag printed on paper, which looked like the kind of paper towels they have in the men's room at the Greyhound Bus Station in Chicago. It had the same symbols he had on his old nasty medallion, which germ-infested thing he stuck back into his pocket. *The Know-Nothing Intelligencer* it was named.

"Why, that's outrageous," Quickskill said. "What fevered brain could have thought that up?"

"Okay, you watch it. Lincoln is courtin destiny. Look how

he went into Richmond like that. Got to be a fool. Going to Richmond before Jeff Davis was fresh out of his chair. It say Lincoln sat in his chair . . . sat in Jefferson Davis' chair, mind you, with a 'serious dreamy look' it say here. Now what kind a fool is that? He is tempting the reaper."

"Listen, ah, 40s, I have to go. I just wanted you to know that Swille knows where we are."

"You come all the way down here to tell me that? Come here." He takes Quickskill to the window. "Look up there." He points to the mountains above the river. "I can hide up there for twenty years and don't have to worry. If you got caught, you wouldn't know what to do. Spent too many years in the Castle. I seed you. Sittin at the piano, turning the pages for the white man, admiring his tune. His eyes highbrow. Yours highbrow. Look like twins. If you had to go to the woods, you wouldn't know what to eat and how to find your way around. You'd eat some mushrooms and die or walk into a bear trap and crush your leg or the elements would get you. No, you let Swille send his dogs, both the four-legged and the two-legged ones. You the one's going to have to hide. I'm already hidin. You don't see me, you don't know me. I'm hidin myself from you right now."

"I . . . I can't understand you guys. You, Leechfield, irrational, bitter. You still see me as a Castle black, some kind of abstraction. If we don't pull together, we are lost."

"I'm not going to put in with no chumps. What do you know? I was with Grant and Lee in Mexico. Bof of em. Mr. Polk's war. They was friends then. We chase Santa Yana's butt all over the mountains. I was there when they captured—"

"In what capacity, a body servant? Fetching eggs for the captain, Arthur Swille the Second, shining his boots and making his coffee? Oh, look, 40s, I'm . . . I didn't want to hurt your feelings. Look . . ." He puts his arm around him.

"Get on way from me."

"But . . ."

"I got all these guns. Look at them. Guns everywhere. Enough to blow away any of them Swille men who come look for me. I don't need no organization. If I was you, Quickskill, I'd forget about this organization."

"Why?"

"Cause them niggers don't wont no organization. You have a organization, they be fighting over which one gone head it; they be fightin about who gone have the money; then they be complainin about things, but when it come down to work, they nowhere to be found. Look, Quickskill, they bring in some women, then it's all over. Then every one of them want to impress the women. They be picking fights with each other and talking louder than each other, then look over at the women, see if they lookin."

"There really doesn't seem to be too much interest in it. Maybe you're right."

40s closed his eyes and rocked in satisfaction. "Now you're talkin, Quickskill. You worry about Quickskill. Leechfield will look after himself, you can be sure of that. Come on, have a drink."

He went to the shelf and pulled a bottle down. It had a mushroom cloud painted on the label. He poured Quickskill a shot glass. He poured himself one. Then he hobbled around the table on his stump. "Here's to the emancipation of our brothers still in bondage, in Virginia, Massachusetts and New York."

They drank. Quickskill's liquor went down. He felt like someone had just shot a hot poker through his navel. Battleships started to move about inside. Gettysburg was inside. His face turned red. He began to choke and his eyes became teary. 40s slapped him on the back.

"How can you drink this stuff?"

"Jersey Lightning. Stuff is good for you. Make your hair grow. Where you think Lincoln got that beard?"

"Yeah, sure," Quickskill said, wheezing and coughing.

"What's going on with Leechfield?"

"He's doing okay. I just left him."

"He's comin up in the world. I saw him in the paper. He had an ad in there. Man, what a con he is."

"Let me see it."

40s rose and got a newspaper from a pile over near the houseboat's one door. He brought it to Quickskill, pointing to Leechfield's ad: "I'll Be Your Slave for One Day." Leechfield was standing erect. In small type underneath the picture it said: "Humiliate Me. Scorn Me."

"This is disgusting."

"Leechfield gets more pussy than a cat, Quickskill. Always driving a long boat. Money."

"What does that Leer have to do with Leechfield?"

"Oh, man, that's his runner."

"I don't get it."

"They pardners. You see, Leer takes photos, and they sell them around the country. It's a mail-order business they got. You'd be surprised how many people enjoy having a slave for a day even when they can't touch them. They say that one of them Radical Republican congressmen even sent for one. Leechfield has come a long way. Use to be nothin but a chicken plucker. That Leer brought him into the big time. First they started out in Tennessee. Leer would pretend to be Leechfield's owner, and he'd have Leechfield dressed up in black cloth pantaloons, black cloth cap, plaided sack coat, cotton check shirt and brogans. And he'd sell Leechfield during the morning and then he'd kidnap Leechfield at night, and then would repeat the same routine to a different buyer the next day. Man, they made a fortune in the nigger-running business. That's how they got the money to come up here."

Quickskill rose.

"You leavin?"

"Yeah, I got to go."

"You upset about Leechfield?"

"Yeah, a little. The slaves really used to look up to him."

"Well, be careful, Quickskill. Swille ain't going to spend all of that time chasing us. He's busy. How'd he find out we were here, anyway?

"It's my poem. You don't understand."

"You got to be kiddin. Words. What good is words?"

"Words built the world and words can destroy the world, 40s."

"Well, you take the words; give me the rifle. That's the only word I need. R-i-f-l-e. Click."

13

Book titles tell the story. The original subtitle for *Uncle Tom's Cabin* was "The Man Who Was a Thing." In 1910 appeared a book by Mary White Ovington called *Half a Man.* Over one hundred years after the appearance of the Stowe book, *The Man Who Cried I Am,* by John A. Williams, was published. Quickskill thought of all of the changes that would happen to make a "Thing" into an "I Am." Tons of paper. An Atlantic of blood. Repressed energy of anger that would form enough sun to light a solar system. A burnt-out black hole. A cosmic slave hole.

Here he was at a White House reception. All of the furniture in the room is worth more than he is. It seems to be sneering at him. The slave waiters look him up and down and cover their grins with their hands. He isn't in the same class as the property. Is there a brotherhood of property? Is he related to the horse, the plow, the carriage? He had just passed the reception line. Shook hands with Lincoln.

Lincoln whispered a rhyme to him that was popular among the slaves and that had fallen into the mouths of the Planters. Generals of the Union had captured it as contraband, and now it was being uttered in the highest circles in Washington:

"If de debble do not ketch
Jeff Davis, dat infernal wretch
An roast and frigazee dat rebble
Wat is de use of any Debble?"

Raven exchanged nervous smiles with the President, and after
he passed he heard the President whisper to an aide, "How did
I do?"

Lincoln was uggggly! An uggggly man. The story was that
Mary Todd Lincoln had become furious at his carryings-on
with Mrs. Charles Griffin, who had inspected the troops with
him, the incident that got tongues to wagging and made Mary
furious, but how could she be jealous of Abe, poor ugly Abe?
Why was he doing this? Inviting artists, writers, dancers and
musicians to the White House?

Quickskill couldn't forget the telegram: "For your poem
'Flight to Canada,' a witty, satiric and delightful contribution
to American letters, we invite you to a White House reception
honoring the leading scribes of America."

Walt Whitman was there. He had written a poem called
"Respondez," in which he had recommended all manner of
excesses: lunatics running the asylum, jailers running the jail.
"Let murderers, bigots, fools, unclean persons offer new propo-
sitions!" And now, here he was as Lincoln's guest in the White
House.

In the same poem he had written: "Let nothing remain
but the ashes of teachers, artists, moralists, lawyers and learned
and polite persons." I guess he was talking about himself,
Quickskill thought, because there he was, as polite as he could
be, grinning, shaking the hands of dignitaries.

Whitman had described Lincoln as "dark brown." Whitman was accurate about that. He stood in the corner for most
of the party, sniffing a lilac.

There were a couple of anti-war scribes that Quickskill
recognized. They were from New York. There was a large
anti-war movement in New York. In fact, New Yorkers were
seriously considering a proposal to secede from the Union for

the purpose of forming a new state: Tri-Insula—Manhattan, Long Island, Staten Island. Some of the New Yorkers were cussing loud, dropping their ashes on the White House rug and picking fights with people.

Raven felt woozy. The night before, flying down to Washington, he had shared a little ale in one of the taverns down on Vesey Street frequented by the anti-slavery, or "free," crowd. He hadn't gotten much sleep.

He clutched his stomach where the pain grabbed him. He began to sweat all over. It must have been the rich lunch they had thrown for the visiting "scribes," as they called them. He was never too hot on French food. He could even eat slave-ship food: salt beef, pork, dried peas, weevily biscuits. But French food always made him sick.

Lincoln's wife Mary was wandering about the room. She was dressed in a white satin evening gown trimmed with black lace. Some military man was escorting her. She shook hands with writers coolly. Todd Lincoln tapped him on the shoulder. It *was* Todd Lincoln. Rumor had it that he was a bigger lush than his old man.

"Anything wrong, Mr. Quickskill?"

"Oh, nothing, Mr. Lincoln, I . . ."

"You know, I enjoyed the poem 'Flight to Canada.' You really laid that Swille planter out. Such wit. Such irony. You're a national institution."

"I . . . I . . ." He was about to collapse.

"Something is wrong?" Todd hurried over to where Lincoln was discussing something with Mathew Brady and whispered in his ear. They looked over his way. He was trying not to make a scene. Lincoln said something back. Todd returned to Quickskill.

"Dad said you could lie down in his bedroom. He never uses it anyway."

"You mean the Lincoln bedroom?"

"Sure, think nothing of it."

14

It was sipping from a glass of wine and listening to the radio. Some new group with a fife, drum, flute. A lot of snare— rap-a-tap tap. Nice. *It* puts the glass back on the rosewood rococo-revival table. *It* is lying in the bed that matches the table. *It* feels better, and now *its* head is swimming, not from the sickness, which has left, but from the occasion. *It* is lying in the President's bed, just as in "Flight to Canada" *it* bragged about lying in Swille's bed. The poem had gotten *it* here. The poem had placed *it* in this place of majesty, of the great, talking and drinking with the creative celebrities of the country.

The poem had also pointed to where *it*, 40s, Stray Leechfield were hiding. Did that make the poem a squealer? A tattler? What else did this poem have in mind for *it. Its* creation, but in a sense, Swille's bloodhound.

It put *its* hands behind *its* head and was lying in the soft pillows and clean sheets. There was a noise in the hall. *It* heard one man talking loud, and the other in a high-pitched squeaky voice—the President.

"But you told me that I ought to get some culture, and so I decided to try to win over the intellectuals in the Eastern establishment who've constantly written Op-eds about my lack of style; now that some of them are here, they are commenting on the beauty of my prose, in between drinks. That's a favorable sign, don't you think?"

"I don't care, Lanky," Swille said. "That shine is my property. I paid good money for him, and you yourself, you said . . ."

"I know, I know. But, Mr. Swille, if you bag him, would you mind carrying him out the back way? If it reaches the newspapers that a fugitive was taken from the very White House, the Radical Republicans, the Abolitionists and the anti-slavery people will call for my impeachment."

Quickskill rubbed his eyes. He hadn't returned to the house for fear of running into the Tracers. He took a sparsely furnished apartment in the Manumit Inn. His bed was a bunk with institution sheets and blankets. That was some dream. The dream was accurate, too, for those who could read dreams. Three years since the Emancipation Proclamation, and it wasn't doing him any good. Swille was an empire unto himself, the Uncrowned King of America, as they were beginning to call him. Swille's law, that's what the Nebraska Tracers cared about. Swille wasn't in the international editions of the *Tribune.* In fact, Swille wasn't in the newspapers much at all any more, since Lincoln had proclaimed Emancipation. Rumors were coming from behind the huge sinister walls of Swille's Castle that the old man had cursed Lincoln's name and was said to be acting in an "inappropriate manner."

People didn't know whether Ms. Swille was dead or alive.

The South was in shambles after Sherman's march. Sherman said that he would "make Georgia howl," and Georgia had howled indeed. The only people Quickskill could convince that Swille was after him were 40s and Leechfield. Leechfield seemed flippant about the matter. Did he actually believe that Swille would accept money from him?

Quickskill went to the window. He didn't see any Southern license plates on the cars. Maybe it was safe. They seemed like gentlemen, but what would they do next? He'd heard of fugitive slaves put in trunks, sacks, in the back of wagons, blindfolded, gagged as they were returned to their Masters. Some were put on trains and others were brought back in elegant buggies in which the slaves were entrapped. Watch out for elegant buggies.

The South is strange. Some of the slaves are leaving the plantations, and some do not desire to leave at all. They are even following the Mistress from town to town. Strange indeed. A mystery.

Quickskill turns on the radio. That Union station in nearby Detroit is playing some patriotic music. It couldn't have been a Union band. The Confederate bands sounded snappy, tight, measured, and played with precision. They were playing this song called "Dixie" with the strange lyrics. The Union bands were rag-taggle.

He dressed and went to the neighborhood of the house he was watching. There weren't any cars in front. He put his collars up about him and walked past the house. Nobody was inside. He went up to the porch, picked up the mail, which was always marked *Forward Please,* it seemed. There was some junk mail and another letter on some stationary made of expensive cloth. It was from *Beulahland Review.* He had sent in a poem; but that was three years ago. They wrote they were going to publish his poem, just as the Nebraska Tracers had said. Hey, they didn't tell him all of it. Two hundred dollars. Two hundred dollars! He could go to Canada. He leaped into the air, throwing his hand behind his head, clutching the letter. Goooooodddd Daaannnngggg! Goooddddd Leeeeee. He was going to CANADA.

Back at Manumit Inn he was lying in bed, daydreaming about himself and some fine suffragette dining on a terrace of a hotel, gazing at the American Falls, and he was about to say, "You're the most beautiful fan I've run into." The phone rang. He picked it up.

"Quickskill?" It was Carpenter. He recognized the voice. Carpenter built red barns and log cabins.

"Yeah, Carpenter. How did you know I was here . . . ?"

"These two dudes from Nebraska was at your house, and they said you'd gone to the john and didn't come back. They said they'd figured you'd be at the Manumit Hotel and asked me to tell you not to make things difficult. What did they mean by that?"

"Skip it, Carpenter. What's up?"

"I'm going to Canada, so I thought I'd throw a little jubilee party."

"You too? My poem, I won a poem, I mean my poem is being published. They're going to give me two hundred dollars. Soon as I get the check, I'm leaving."

"Great! Maybe I'll see you there. I'm leaving tomorrow."

"Maybe so."

"Well, be sure to come to my party. We begin at about seven."

"I'll be there." He hung up. Carpenter could go and come back. He was a free Negro, and had been free for some years. He had what they called a "viable" trade. He had bought the freedom of his mother and his wife. Free. Quickskill thought about it. A freedom writer, never again threatened with "Ginny." His poems were "readings" for him from his inner self, which knew more about his future than he did.

While others had their tarot cards, their ouija boards, their I-Ching, their cowrie shells, he had his "writings." They were his bows and arrows. He was so much against slavery that he had begun to include prose and poetry in the same book, so that there would be no arbitrary boundaries between them. He preferred Canada to slavery, whether Canada was exile, death, art, liberation, or a woman. Each man to his own Canada. There was much avian imagery in the poetry of slaves. Poetry about dreams and flight. They wanted to cross that Black Rock Ferry to freedom even though they had different notions as to what freedom was.

They often disagreed about it, Leechfield, 40s. But it was his writing that got him to Canada. "Flight to Canada" was responsible for getting him to Canada. And so for him, freedom was his writing. His writing was his HooDoo. Others had their way of HooDoo, but his was his writing. It fascinated him, it possessed him; his typewriter was his drum he danced to.

15

Carpenter noticed him as soon as he entered the house. He left the circle of guests around him and ran up to Quickskill.

"Man, I can't wait. I'm going to hit all the spots in Toronto. I got this fine suite reserved for me in the King Edward Hotel. It's advertised in *The New York Times*. 'A Gracious Tradition' it says in the ad. I'm going to get me a good night's sleep and get up and order me some breakfast. I'm going to have me some golden pancakes and maple syrup, bacon, sausage, ham—I'm going to have all three. Then I'm going to have some marmalade and a big old glass of grapefruit juice. That's how I'm going to start out. Then I'm going to take in the sights. Up there the Plantation House is just something on display at the Toronto Museum. Don't have to worry about who's my friend and who's my enemy, like it is here. Anybody might turn out to be crazy, I'm always mistaken for a fugitive sl— I . . . I . . ."

"That's all right, Carpenter. You know, I'll be joining you soon."

"When you coming up?"

"Soon as I receive the check from the magazine."

"Man, I'm glad. I didn't know that writing paid."

"Yeah, well . . ."

"Hey, Quickskill, I did a poem once. Maybe you'd look at it. It's not as professional as your work but maybe you can introduce me to one of them big-time editors and . . ."

"I'm busy right now. Maybe when I get to Canada, maybe then."

"Yeah, sure, Quickskill. There's plenty of time. Think I might crowd out your gig, huh, Quickskill?"

"Sure, Carpenter, sure." Quickskill managed a weak smile. There was always an air of condescension in the way free slaves related to fugitive slaves. Especially the ones from Louisiana. He was never able to figure that out. The slavemasters in Louisiana often freed their sons by African women. Some of these children became slave owners themselves. But some of them in Emancipation, seeing that there was some money to be made in anti-slavery lecturing, often mounted the platform and talked about their treatment from hickory whips, lashes made of rawhide strands, so convincingly, it was difficult to tell the real sufferers from the phony ones. Carpenter wasn't like that, though. He had a trade. He could find work anywhere.

"Look, Quickskill," Carpenter said from that round face which exuded warmth and friendship, "come on in and make yourself comfortable. What did you bring?"

"I brought some Paul Lawrence Dunbar cuisine."

"Out-of-sight, man. Take it into the kitchen."

Carpenter returned to his guests. Quickskill entered the parlor in Carpenter's shotgun house.

They were playing some kind of old-style Spanish dance; the women were wearing flowers behind their ears and doing fancy dips and turns, while the old men wore their mellow California hats, slanted. There was some bending back and some elegant freezes going on; weaving of invisible nets with fingers. Some of the local Native American poets were there too, standing in a huddle, drinking Coke. In the dining room men were standing around a table, smoking cigars and discussing the Emancipation.

They began to smile when they spotted Quickskill laying down his contribution to the slave food that was on the table.

Dunbar food: wheat bread, egg pone, hog jaws, roasted shoat, ham sliced cold. He had brought some Beaujolais, which he placed down next to the dishes of meat, fish and the variety of salad with Plantation dressing. Somebody else had brought John Brown à la carte—boiled beef, cabbage, pork and beans. The bottles of champagne looked chilled and ready to pop their tops.

He returned to the main room, where the guests were dancing. Leechfield was in the middle of the room doing a mean Walk-Around with this long-legged stack of giggles, who was dancing around like a tranquilized ostrich. Quickskill recognized her as the Abolitionist principal of the Free High School. Due to her New England Abolitionist ideas about education, some of the slave children had become, under her influence, surly and unmanageable, wouldn't mind their parents and referred to themselves as the future; 1900s people, they were calling themselves. Leechfield, a little grey in his beard and with those squint devilish eyes, was enjoying himself. He hopped into Chicken Wings and ended it up with some dance they were doing called the Copperhead. His partner was trying to keep up, bouncing about and moving her bony elbows like a mutant ape.

The front door opened, admitting a new guest: Princess Quaw Quaw Tralaralara. She was the frontier dancer, an accurate-shooting, limb-wriggling desperado; tear a man's nose off. She could put the palms of her feet on the top of your bush, so limber was she. She was extremely good doing limber things. She wore Western boots, denims. She recognized Quickskill and began that smile that made you feel that the top of your brain pan was coming off. You could put the tip of your tongue along the roof of her mouth and feel like Pinocchio inside some soft whale, spouting and leaping in the Atlantic. She could stand ten feet away from you and make you feel that she was all over you. She was a real mountain climber. She was popular on the college circuit, performing Indian dances.

She approached him, hips moving like those of a woman who swims fifty laps a day and subsists on bananas and yogurt.

"Quickskill," she said, in one of her Anglicized sentences, "it's so nice to see you. It's been such a long time. Fort Thunderbird?"

Fort Thunderbird was where the fugitive slaves obtained their Emancipation papers as soon as they arrived in Emancipation City. It was a complex of buildings called "Jack's Plaza," built by her husband, Yankee Jack the pirate, or rather consultant on trade routes and compiler of shipping logs, as his business card read. He was somewhat of a hero in these parts because of his condemnation of those pirates who pirated human cargo. He was even more indignant over the fact that they kept bogus logs so as to deceive the British Navy. He considered them to be untidy. He was a respectable pirate, and so he only dealt in things like distribution, abandoning taking over trade routes and shanghaiing ships as crude. He also dabbled in jewels, gold and real estate.

He was dedicating his life to building Emancipation City, a refuge for slaves, Indians and those who committed heinous acts because society made them do it. This Wordsworth reader, connoisseur of good wines, good theatre, good art and other finer things of life was known around these parts as the Good Pirate. And when he took as his bride Quaw Quaw, cultured performer of Ethnic Dance, finer than Pocahontas, sturdy as the Maid of the Mist—actually married this Third World belle, since heathen women were available to pirates under any condition the pirate wanted—when he actually put a ring on her finger, there was a celebration for days. Neighboring tribes attended. And when his church objected to this marriage between a Christian and an Infidel, he closed the church down, so to this day there's no church in Emancipation City, just various temples of different religions where people wander in and out. Some are near the city parks, others right downtown. He was a worldly pirate, but Raven Quickskill had learned how to read between the lines in his job of preparing slave invoices. He had something on this pirate. Something . . . something awful! Something everybody knew but Quaw Quaw. No one had the heart to tell her. Quickskill had written an unpublished poem about it. A rare "serious" love poem for him.

When Raven first came to town, he checked in at the general store where the registration was going on; he could see the pirates' castle on a mountain overlooking Pirates' Plaza. It was a replica of Crevecoeur (heartbreak), the slave fort built by the Europeans on the coast of Guinea. After having his papers signed, he bought some stamps, writing paper and typewriter ribbon. He then decided to take a tour of the slave castle. The tour cost a penny.

He got lost from the main tour group and mistakenly entered an upstairs room, where Quaw Quaw lay in an old French bed underneath a canopy. She had her knees drawn up and was reading a chapbook. The poems of a New Englander. They were about lobsters, aunts and religion.

"Oh, I didn't mean to interrupt you. I got lost from the main tour," Quickskill said.

"Raven Quickskill," she said.

She recognized him as the fugitive slave writer. She was always haunting the bookstalls. Next to her bed was a tray of cherrystones, eggs benedict, a tall glass of grapefruit juice and a pot of coffee. She invited him to pull up a chair next to her bed and talk to her about poetry. She had begun to back up poets at public readings with her dances. He told her about the poem he was working on, "Flight to Canada," and how he had submitted it to *Beulahland Review.*

She talked about her husband and what a good man he was, even though some people libeled him by calling him a pirate; and she talked about how her husband, the pirate, had taught her to see: "I mean, really see."

And before you knew it, they were in bed together, in this slave castle, in this warm bed covered with silk-laced blankets; in this slave castle, floors above where his ancestors rotted in chains, in this pirate's bed, in this slave castle with its stone floors and knights' statues. A portrait of her husband done in Rembrandt style hung above them.

Was she a roadrunner? It was hard for her to catch up,

but he wouldn't call her a turtle because when she did catch up he had to hold on to her cheeks as though they were Spirit-of-St.-Louis' seats in Lindbergh's plane, the only thing between him and the Atlantic. Then it was rodeo; a lot of bucking and slipping out. It had gone that way for some time until they had fallen out of touch. They had an argument about the Kansas-Nebraska Act. She said that slavery was a state of mind, metaphysical. He told her to shut the fuck up.

"I'm glad to see you, Quaw Quaw; it's been a few years." She stared at him, waiting for him to hurt her, but he wasn't going to. "I see you're backing up that pirate, Captain Kidd, and his translations of Oceanic poetry. You're a good dancer, what are you performing behind this character for?"

He was missing her. It showed when he was missing her. Sometimes they had drunk wine together in a café at a table covered with red-and-white-checkered cloth, where the bread was served in woven baskets. They'd rendezvous every time her husband went to those conventions on trade routes he was always attending. Sometimes he was in New York, looking in on his galleries and jewelry stores.

"It's none of your business, Raven. Times have changed. I'm not your squaw any more. And speaking of squaw, Captain Kidd was the hit of the Squaw Valley writers' conference last year. People just adored his translations."

She was getting mad. She was spoiled, often swimming all the way out, teasing the undercurrent of things. She played hard and came from a line of lean, hard players. Her father fought the U.S. Cavalry to a draw. Her grandfather never made peace with the white man and never surrendered and is remembered by a high boulder which sits in the middle of the Colorado River. The only real hard thing he knew about her were her nipples, hot little plums when his tongue would dart over there and give them instructions. When he was lizard-licking those titties, she'd grunt then. "You're just not broad enough, Quickskill. You're . . . you're too . . . too ethnic. You should be more universal. More universal."

"How can I be universal with a steel collar around my

neck and my hands cuffed all the time and my feet bound? I can't be universal, gagged. Look, Quaw Quaw, they want your Indian; that's what they want, and you're giving it to them. You're the exotic of the new feudalism. For what Camelot can't win on the battlefield it'll continue in poetry. Nobody starts a war with poetry for fear of being made to look like a philistine. Look, I dip my spoon into the pot. Sometimes my shoestrings break, and I go a long time without buying new ones. I'm coarse, I'm rude, but that's the democrat's style. That's why they're calling Abe the Illinois Ape. He's standing up to them. The South can't continue Camelot. That's what it's all about. Effete men leaving the management of their plantations to uncles; the women playthings; popinjays partying endlessly, flowery waistcoats. And their poetry—gentlemen's gardening triviality. If they love birds so much, why are they killing them off? But your friends, and their exotic dabbling—their babbas, their yogi—are on the same trip. They're going to get your Indian and my Slave on microfilm and in sociology books; then they're going to put them in a space ship and send them to the moon. And then they're going to put you on the nickel and put me on a stamp, and that'll be the end of it. They're as Feudalist and Arthurian as Davis, but whereas he sees it as a political movement, they see it as a poetry movement."

"There you go with that race stuff again. Politics. Race. People write and paint about politics because they have nothing else to say."

"You're so fucking glib. People have nothing else to do my ass. You've been hanging out with the Apostles of Aesthetics and you like them because you think they want to put you in a tower and fight dragons over you. You don't look like Guenevere to me. You want some punk to strum on a mandolin some old knightly song while you flutter your eyes and sip martinis. Well, drat your universality. We slaves don't have time to be sitting around on velvet-cushioned couches contemplating 'dragonflies moving with the wings of gauze' all day and shit."

"Oh, you wouldn't understand. You're so . . . so savage."

He turned around and hurried away. He glanced at Carpenter in the front room and pumped his hand. "Maybe I'll run into you in Canada," he said, but Carpenter didn't hear him.

He was about to open the white picket gate when Quaw Quaw called, "Don't be mad, Quickskill. Don't leave so soon. I was just trying to communicate."

"Communicate what?"

"You know how non-verbal I am."

"I don't get you. Listen, I have to go home and pack."

"Pack? You taking a trip, Quickskill?"

"Yeah, I'm going to Canada."

"Is that a permanent move?"

When he said yes, there was a glint of sadness in her eyes. Sure, they had discontinued their playing around, but it was nice to know that they were in the same town.

She started to pout, real cute, though she got all suffragette and curt when he called her "cute." She held her hands behind her back and began to look disappointed. "Quickskill, there's a den downstairs; let's go down and have a drink. There's a television set. I will never forget how much you like television. You would keep it on without even looking at it."

"I'm glad to know it's there. The world will disappear if it's not there."

"Come on, Quickskill." She led him by the hand.

"I can't stay long."

They entered the house and walked back, passing Carpenter and his guests.

They made drinks in the den. She had a double vodka on the rocks with a twist of lemon; he, some red wine. He got up and turned on the television set. This was a nice room that Carpenter had made in the basement of his house. Around the walls were photos of African architecture. There was a conference table where he held meetings for his Carpenter Company. They restored log cabins. Not the usual log cabins but ones with space and light; peaceful log cabins. There was an educational television play on. It was being presented live from

Washington. The opening shots showed dignitaries arriving. Searchlights. The carriages were pulling up, and people were standing outside the Ford Theatre.

The play's audience was giving President Lincoln a standing ovation; his white wife, Mary Todd, stood next to him. They were beaming. He could see her eyes glistening. People in Emancipation liked her. A most unusual First Lady. She said what was on her mind, sometimes embarrassing her husband.

The audience was applauding wildly. Lincoln, a twinkle in his eyes, was waving back.

"It's the President," Quaw Quaw said. "That hick. I didn't know he went in for culture. I read in *The Realist* that back in Illinois he operated a still. You should have heard the way my professors at Columbia talked about him. They made fun of his Corn Belt accent and that stupid stovepipe. They are so urbane. Many of them have published poems in *The New Yorker.*

"Yeah, they all read as if they were written in a summer home on Long Island, about three o'clock in the morning, with many things yet unpacked."

She stood up, balling her fist. "Now, they're wonderful writers. How dare you attack my sensibilities? This race talk all the time . . ."

"You'll never change. Daughter of the West. Pocahontas rushing to place her body between the white man and the arrow intended for him. You and your Anglican Injuns."

"I knew it would be savage out here. My teachers at Columbia said so. I plan to go back there. I miss the teas and hanging out in the bookstalls."

"Camelot. Camelot West, Camelot East, Camelot South. One big fucking Camelot. With darkies and Injuns to set places, pour and serve at the Round Table. Playing on the lute and reciting verse, doing court dances. Do you know how your husband treats that swami he's bought? He's nothing but a houseboy. 'Vill Mr. Jack need somring?' 'Is Mr. Jack's footrest not high?' He locks him in a closet, and told the dog trainer to sniff the swami's clothes in case the swami got ideas. When the swami did manage to free himself and found a phone, he tried to get some poets to organize a benefit for him, only to discover that your husband, Yankee Jack, had warned them if they tried to help him, he'd cut off their grant money. He can't even raise carfare to return to India, the poor chap. And that's not all, there's rumors going around what he's done to you, I . . . I . . ."

"What rumors, Quickskill?"

"Oh, I . . . don't want to say."

"Quickskill, you generalize so."

"Come on, Quaw Quaw, let's stop arguing." He grabbed her hand. He was pulling her toward the sofa. She was between him and the television set. He could hear from the stillness of the audience that Tom Tyler's new play was about to begin.

She was resisting. "It's been a long time, Raven. I have to get used to you again."

Before he knew it he had a tiny nipple in his mouth. Her sweater was pulled up about her neck. It was a soft purring sweater made of lamb's wool, a rose-colored sweater. She was wearing some kind of hip Bohemian college-women's scent, Bonnard '60. The kind of women who studied under teachers who scolded them for not being able to identify more than twenty-five spices, or not being able to walk right. They never walked splayfooted and bowlegged, with their necks lowered. It had a French name—posture.

DUN: Miss Florence, will you be kind enough to tell Miss Georgina all about that American relative of yours.

FLO: Oh, about my American cousin; certainly. *(Aside to Harry)* Let's have some fun. Well, he's about seventeen feet high.

DUN: Good gracious! Seventeen feet high!

FLO: They are all seventeen feet high in America, ain't they, Mr. Vernon?

VER: Yes, that's about the average height.

FLO: And they have long black hair that reaches down to their heels; they have dark copper-colored skin, and they fight with— What do they fight with, Mr. Vernon?

VER: Tomahawks and scalping knives.

FLO: Yes; and you'd better take care, Miss Georgina, or he'll take his tomahawk and scalping knife and scalp you immediately.

He let his tongue linger there for a while, darting, taking long agonizing strokes, moving like a feather.

ASA: There was no soft soap.

DE B: Soft soap!

AUG: Soft soap!

VER: Soft soap!

MRS. M: Soft soap!

FLO: Soft soap!

GEO *(on sofa)*: Soft soap!

DUN: Thoft Thoap?

ASA: Yes, soft soap. I reckon you know what that is. However, I struck a pump in the kitchen, slicked my hair down a little, gave my boots a lick of grease, and now I feel quite handsome; but I'm everlastingly dry.

FLO: You'll find ale, wine and luncheon on the side table.

ASA: Wal, I don't know as I've got any appetite. You see, comin along on the cars I worried down half a dozen ham sandwiches, eight or ten boiled eggs, two or three pumpkin pies and a strong of cold sausages—and— Wal, I guess I can hold on till dinnertime.

DUN: Did that illustrious exile eat all that? I wonder where he put it.

ASA: I'm as dry as a sap-tree in August.

Her head was lying back. Her black hair was hanging over the couch. His dick was hard and was trying to break out of his pants. He had removed that left white cup from over her breast mound, and now his fingers moved the other white cup up. And he slithered across her chest till he reached that one. Then he went to town, his free finger bringing down that zipper. "Oh, Quickskill," she was saying. "Oh, Quickskiiiillll." She'd draw it out. His finger moved underneath her short white panties, which were embroidered around the edges with lily designs. He dug that, the contrast. Those denims and those panties. The denims now down over her ankles.

She started breathing real hard; he was, too, and she helped relieve him by zipping down his pants and taking out his dick. She was moving the brown skin up and down with her hand. He was moving his finger into the vagina crescent. They started to move in a seesaw fashion. Then there was some hip-swiveling and bending backwards.

AUG: Oh, Mr. Trenchard, why did you not bring me one of those lovely Indian's dresses of your boundless prairie?

MRS. M: Yes, one of those dresses in which you hunt the buffalo.

AUG *(extravagantly)*: Yes, in which you hunt the buffalo.

ASA *(imitating)*: In which I hunt the buffalo. *(Aside)* Buffaloes down in Vermont. *(Aloud)* Wal, you see, them dresses are principally the nateral skin, tipped off with paint, and the Indians object to parting with them.

She got up and took her clothes off, threw them on a chair, removed the pins from her hair and let it down. He was trembling, removing his shoes. He was always trembling at this point. He would tie his shoelaces in knots, or he'd spend time trying to put his clothes in one place so that he wouldn't be missing a sock or having his host find the wrong thing underneath his couch or caught under the seat of a chair.

FLO: What's that, sir? Do you want to make me jealous?

ASA: Oh, no, you needn't get your back up, you are the right sort too, but you must own you're small potatoes, and few in a hill compared to a gal like that.

FLO: I'm what?

ASA: Small potatoes.

FLO: Will you be kind enough to translate that for me, for I don't understand American yet.

ASA: Yes, I'll put it in French for you, *"petites pommes de terre."*

The lights went out. The television light was the only one in the room. It gave out a bluish haze.

ASA: Yes, about the ends they're as black as a nigger's in billing time, and near the roots they're all speckled and streaked.

DUN *(horror-struck)*: My whiskers speckled and streaked?

ASA *(showing bottle)*: Now, this is a wonderful invention.

DUN: My hair dye. My dear sir.

ASA *(squeezing his hand)*: How are you?

DUN: Dear Mr. Trenchard.

He could see her round red back reflected in the television screen. He was holding on to her. They were moving up and down. She was holding him around the neck. What they must mean when they say "cleaving." He clove. She clove. She was in his mind; he in hers.

ASA: Wal, I guess shooting with bows and arrows is just about like most things in life, all you've got to do is to keep the sun out of your eyes, look straight—pull strong—calculate the distance, and you're sure to hit the mark in most things . . .

They were as complex as the hedges trimmed by the Royal Gardener of London. They were underneath in a subaqueous city. If the Devil had reared this city, then the Devil was better than God. That's why God always maintained a dour expression and the Devil was grinning all the time. This primitive act made them behave like children, and they began to giggle and tease and play hide and seek. There was a lot of hiding and seeking and seeking and hiding. They reached the hilt and then . . .

        *   *   *

ASA: . . . You sockdologizing old mantrap!
Screams.

"What's the matter, Quickskill?" she whispered.

The cameras were focused upon the President's box. Lincoln lay slumped to his left side, his arm dangling. The assassin must have been a Southerner, because he was dressed to kill. And before he hobbled off the stage he struck one of those old theatrical poses; his slicked hair gleaming, his weak spine curved, a hand to his chest, he yelled, *"Sic semper Tyrannis"* and "Revenge for the South." Quickskill sat staring into the set; Quaw Quaw, aghast, her hand shielding her mouth, sitting next to him. Somebody from the party played around with the doorknob to the den, but then, realizing that it was locked, joined the commotion coming from the other room of this "Good Friday" party.

Quickskill recognized the famous actor who just a few weeks before had played Antony to the Cassius of Junius Brutus Booth and the Brutus of Edwin Booth, to "lavish applause of the audience mingled with the waving of handkerchiefs, and every mark of enthusiasm."

Booth, America's first Romantic Assassin. They replay the actual act, the derringer pointing through the curtains, the President leaning to one side, the First Lady standing, shocked, the Assassin leaping from the balcony, gracefully, beautifully, in slow motion. They promise to play it again on the Late News. When the cameras swing back to the balcony, Miss Laura Keene of *Our American Cousin* is at Lincoln's side "live." Her gown is spattered with brain tissue. A reporter has a microphone in Mary Todd's face.

"Tell us, Mrs. Lincoln, how do you feel having just watched your husband's brains blown out before your eyes?"

"Oh, turn it off," Quaw Quaw says, holding her hands over her ears. "How can you watch that thing?"

They went out of the den. Back to the party. Some of the people who had often called Lincoln a "gorilla" and a "baboon" were now weeping in the arms of others. Some of the women were screaming. Others were huddled about a television set, watching the latest developments. He walked out of the party with Quaw Quaw.

As they drove toward Yankee Jack's castle, people could be seen in the streets, weeping. Some were listening to their transistors. Crowds of people were standing on the corner, waiting for the papers. They reached her husband's grounds, a huge gate with secret symbols carved on it. There was the wall surrounding it. Behind the gates he could see some of the Orientals sitting under trees, arms outstretched, eyes closed. Others were walking back and forth in monk's robes in "meditation." She got out of the car. Her eyes were red.

Before entering the gate, she paused and turned to Quickskill, who was sitting in his sedan. "When are you leaving for Canada, Quickskill?"

"As soon as the check arrives from *Beulahland Review.* That'll pay for transportation. They set up a reading for me, too. The Anti-Slavery Society of Western New York. They said they could get someone with a yacht to take me across the Niagara River into Canada."

"Take me with you, Raven! Please take me with you!"

"But—"

"This country is violent, just like my Columbia professors said. They said it had no salvation. They said they didn't expect most of us to live out our lives in this cacophonous rat trap. Ezra Pound was right. 'A half-savage country.' That's what it is, a half-savage country. Every time someone in E.P.'s circle spoke American he was fined a dollar."

"He hardly ever spent time in this 'half-savage country,' " Quickskill observed. "His mind was always someplace else. That was his problem, his mind was away somewhere in a feudal tower. Eliot, too. The Fisher King. That's Arthurian. How can anybody capture the spirit of this 'half-savage country' if they don't stay here? Poetry is knowing. When I wrote 'Flight to Canada' it was poetry, but it was poetry based upon something I knew. I don't even see how you can call them Union poets. They hated America. Eliot hated St. Louis. How can someone hate St. Louis? How the fuck can someone hate St. Louis? I mean, W. C. Handy; the Jefferson Arc. They were Royalists."

"Quickskill, let's stop arguing. Take me with you to Canada. I won't do the evening of Oceanic poetry with Captain Kidd. I'll never perform on the stage again. Not here. This . . . this unholy savage ground. Assassins and mobs. Gong-banging. It's a rowdy roundhouse. I need to be somewhere refined. Why, they speak French in Quebec. I'll be like Blondin."

"Who is this Blondin? Another avant-garde racket? You and your friends have turned the avant-garde into a racket."

"Oh, you never care about what I'm interested in. My world. You're never interested in that. All you talk about is slavery. Kansas, Nebraska, Dred Scott, Manumit. Dumb words like that. Manumit. The chain around your ankle; the cowhide on your back; the bloodhound teethmarks on your ass. I'm sick of it. You and your stupid slavery. You and your stupid slavery can go hang. Go to Canada. See if I care. I hope it's a real bad bummer."

He'd often forget how young she was. "Quaw Quaw . . ."

She was heading up the path toward the pirate's castle and would not heed his call.

"Quaw Quaw."

She kept walking, her buttocks moving from left to right, her hair on the sides of her face like hairy blinders. Her arms were folded. She was looking down.

"Quaw Quaw Tralaralara."

She turned. She had her hands on her hips.

"Meet me at the dock tomorrow. The steamer leaves at ten."

She jumped up and down like a schoolgirl playing volley ball. She turned around and ran up the path, her arms flying in front of her. Quickskill started up the motor. The car moved back down the mountain toward Emancipation's center.

He said that he wouldn't give any more, but when she put

it that way, when she started pouting . . . He once called her an emotional anarchist bomb. She was a love terrorist. You didn't know when she was going off. Maybe that's why she was a dancer. He said he'd never give into her again, but when she started pouting and when she rolled those beautiful dark eyes at him, he gave and he gave and he gave and gave. Charm, the physicists say, is real.

Man is in the last stage of his evolution. Women will be here.

16

". . . and also, Robin, don't forget to order a few more cartons of Crisco. We seem to be always running out."

Uncle Robin is mounted on Swille's personal beautifully gold-harnessed horse, Beauvoir, rumored to have sired both Lee's horse Traveller and Davis' Tartar. It was doing a fancy Spanish trot in place. Uncle Robin wears a silk top hat, riding jacket, white silk ascot, long black boots, and holds a whip which thickens out into a point like the end of a blacksnake's tail.

"And be careful with that whip, Robin. It's my pride and joy."

"Yessir, Massa Swille."

After sending Robin, followed by the two wagons, to the city for supplies, Swille looks out over his land, six times as big as Monaco. A flock of mockingbirds flies overhead. The lilacs, bordering the path down which Robin's caravan was now leaving, sway slightly; the drawbridge descends.

He turned and opened the door of his house, said to be the very door on Arthur's house in Camelot. The Prime Minister who had traded it as collateral on a personal loan was forced to resign when the deal was discovered by the London *Times*. Attempts to recover it were futile. Swille threatened to make

England giggle into its tea. Swille wanted London Bridge but was overbid by a Texan who later sold it to the Arabs as the Brooklyn Bridge.

He climbed the spiraling staircase on the sensuous plush rugs and entered the second story of the house. He came to his wife's room, put his ear to the door. Silence.

Swille entered his own room. It was time for a "Siesta" he noted by looking at his watch. He walked over to his closet and opened it. "Ah, there they are. Don't they shine? Aren't they wonderful? My lovelies, my darlings, my pets." He takes one of the whips to his bosom and rubs it. *"My cowskin one! A kiss for you! My bullwhip! A caress for you! My chains. My beautiful chains.* If Gladstone could only see these. My paddles."

His collection was better than Gladstone's. Gladstone had invited him to his English country house for a "spanker" and to see his exotic whips and chains, but when he told Gladstone, Lord of the Exchequer, about the collections in the South, Gladstone caused a "sensation" by making a pro-Confederate speech on the floor of Parliament. He urged England to recognize the Confederacy.

Swille removed his jacket, picked up a copy of *The Southern Planter* which had a special edition on the new "fettering" devices. They were all right, but they couldn't compare with his. His had been based upon those described in Henry's *History*, 1805 edition, Volume VII. He had had them shipped over from a deserted English castle. To make sure they were effective, he had Jim, the black stud, try them on him personally. He always tried out the fettering equipment personally so's to determine whether he'd gotten his money's worth. He loved the sound of the screams coming from various parts of the plantation, day and night. Eddie Poe had gone bonkers over his equipment and used some of it in his short stories. He put the book down, walked over to the bed and lay down. He picked up the phone next to the bed.

"Mammy, would you bring me some 'Siesta,' perhaps some of those Tennysonian poppies which were shipped over from the Epicurean Club last week?"

The Epicurean Club was going to recommend his barony at their next meeting. Baron Swille. Or how about Sir Baron Swille? That's too cluttered. Maybe the Marquis d'Swille.

Barracuda entered the room carrying a silver tray in the center of which was a logo of the House of Swille: a belligerent Eagle with whips in its talons. She wore a purple velvet dress with silver hoops, a pongee apron with Belgian lace, and emerald earrings. Lying on the platter was an apothecary bottle full of an emerald-green quivering liquid. Next to this was a hypodermic needle and a syringe. He rolled up his sleeve. Mammy Barracuda put the tray down on the table and prepared the injection. She shot it into Swille's arm. He convulsed slightly. Then he began to babble. "Quite good, quite good, Mammy," he said, wetting his lips.

"Anything else, Arthur?"

"No, Mammy, just tell them to warm up the chopper for my trip. I'll be leaving as soon as my 'Siesta' dissipates."

"All right, Massa Swille." Mammy Barracuda left the room.

He couldn't miss the lecture at the Magnolia Club tonight. Some huge blond brute was speaking. He bent his arm, covered the needle hole with a patch, rolled down his sleeve.

His mind was swimming. I'll fix these Confederates come busting up to my place. Let Lincoln and Davis fight it out like the backwoodsmen they are. Why, that Davis, putting on airs. The Kentucky cabin he was born in had only three more rooms than Abe's. Can't even control his generals. If they'd chased the Yankees after Bull Run like he said, they'd won the war. No, they had to sit around having tea. Let Davis and Lincoln kill each other off, and then during the confusion I'll declare myself King, and, as for Queen, Vivian.

Vivian, my disconsolate damsel, if only you . . . my fair pale sister. Your virgin knees and golden hair in your sepulcher by the sea. Let me creep into your mausoleum, baby. My insatiable Vivian by the sea, remember how we used to go for walks down to the levee and wait for the *Annabel Lee*. You were only fourteen years old, yet ours is a romance of the days that were. You, having difficulty making up your mind whether to "pass" from dismay or despair, me feverishly penning letters tainted with lily oil from my apartment on the Bois de Boulogne. And that night before you died, you were just right. What would I do without our great love, a love as old as Ikhnaton, the royal love, the royal love . . . the royal.

Swille is walking in the clouds in a great city. Floating toward a castle. He comes to a door with Islamic-type designs on it. Can this be? The door opens, and there before him is a great round table at which is seated a brilliant company. Can this be real? Ethiopian minstrels wearing silver collars, silk and embroidery are playing their instruments. And there Vivian sweeps out toward him and puts her hand in his. She is wearing the negligee she "passed" in, and she's singing their favorite song. Fairy bells. Fairy bells. And the King . . . King Arthur says, "Come forth, my children. Baron and Baroness Swille." And they begin to walk as the knights shout, raising their swords and lifting their crystal goblets, "Baron Swille. Baroness Swille."

Barracuda enters the room. She rouses him.

"Barracuda, what on earth's the matter? I'm having my 'Siesta.' I . . ."

"Your 'Siesta' gon have to wait. It's your wife again, Arthur. She looks real Emancipated. Dark circles under the eyes. Peek'd. She say she not going to talk unless she fed intravenous. She say she on strike. All she do now is lay in bed, watch television, read movie books and eat candy. She drinks an awful lot, too, Mr. Swille. She be listening to that Beecher Hour show."

"Well, Mammy, in that case, you know what to do."

"That I do," Barracuda says, rubbing her hands together, "that I do."

17

Barracuda enters the Mistress' room. Surveys the scene. Puts her hands on her hips. The Mistress flutters her eyes. Turns her head toward the door where Barracuda is standing, tapping her foot.

"Oh, Barracuda, there you are, my dusky companion, my comrade in Sisterhood, my Ethiopian suffragette."

"Oooomph," Barracuda says. "Don't choo be sistering me, you lazy bourgeoise skunk."

"Barracuda," the Mistress says, raising up, "what's come over you?"

"What's come ovah me? What's come ovah you, you she-thing? Got a good man. A good man. A powerful good man. And here you is—you won't arrange flowers when his guests come. You won't take care of the menu. You won't do nothing that a belle is raised to do."

"But, Barracuda, Ms. Stowe says . . ."

"I don't care what that old crazy fambly say. They ain't doin nothin but causing a mess. Now it's about time you straighten up."

Barracuda walks over to the bed, takes a box of candy from next to where Ms. Swille is resting, throws it to the floor.

"Barracuda!"

Barracuda ignores her Mistress' pleas and knocks over the whiskey bottle on the stand next to the bed, then throws back the covers.

"Barracuda, I'll catch the flu. I'm always catching the flu."

"Get out dat bed!"

"Why . . . what? What's come over you, Barracuda?"

Barracuda goes to the window and raises it. "This room needs to air out. Oooooomph. Whew!" Barracuda pinches her nose. "What kind of wimmen is you?"

"Why, I'm on strike, Barracuda. I refuse to budge from this bed till my husband treats me better than he treats the coloreds around here."

"Now, I'm gon tell you one mo time. Git out dat bed!"

"Barracuda! This has gone far enough." The Mistress brings back her frail alabaster arm as if to strike Barracuda. Barracuda grabs it and presses it against the bed. "Barracuda! Barracuda! You're hurting me. Oooooo."

Barracuda grabs her by the hair and yanks her to the floor.

"Barracuda, Barracuda, what on earth are you doing to my delicate fragile body. Barracuda!"

Barracuda gives her a kind of football-punt kick to her naked hip, causing an immediate red welt.

"Barracuda, now that's enough, you . . . you impertinent, black Raggedy Ann, you."

Barracuda pulls her razor, bends down and puts it to Ms. Swille's lily-white neck. "You see that, don't you? You know what that is now? Now do what I say."

"Anything you say, Barracuda," Ms. Swille says, sobbing softly.

"BANGALANG.   BANGALLLLAAAANNNNG. YOUUUUUU. WHOOOOOO. BANGALANG." Barracuda, one black foot on Ms. Swille's chest, calls for her assistant.

Bangalang rushes into the room, her pickaninny curls rising up, her hands thrown out at the red palms, her eyes growing big in their sockets at the sight.

"Don't just stand there, girl; go draw some bath water."

Bangalang rushes into the bathroom and begins to draw the water.

"Now get up."

"Barracuda. Barracuuuudaaaaa."

The Missus of the household moans, holding on to Barracuda's skirts. Barracuda knees her in the mouth. She falls back, blood spurting from the wound.

"Now get up, I say!"

She is lying in the middle of the floor, her blondish-streaked orange-grey hair spread out before her, moaning.

"I say get up! Where my poker?" Barracuda goes to the fireplace.

"All right, Barracuda. All right." Ms. Swille slowly rises to her feet.

Barracuda begins to shove her toward the bathroom, where Bangalang has drawn the water. "Now move, you old mothefukin she-dog. You scarecrow. You douche-bag! You flea-sack drawers! You no-tit mother of a bloodhound. You primary chancre! Get on in there, like Barracuda say." She keeps shoving her. "Look like shit. On strike. I got your strike, you underbelly of a fifteen-pound gopher rat run ober by a car. Sleep with a dog, he let you. You goat-smelling virago, you gnawing piranha, worrying that man like that." She shoves her into the bathroom and the woman slips and falls because Bangalang has caused the tub to overflow. "What da matta . . . Fool!"

"You tole me to turn it on; you didn't say anything about turning it off," Bangalang says in her Topsy voice.

"Where my . . . ?"

But before Barracuda could find an appropriate weapon, Bangalang, the little pickaninny, has dashed from under her skirts and out of the room. Ms. Swille lies in the water on the floor, unconscious. Barracuda picks her up as though she were a child and throws her into the tub. She lies there face down, until she begins to gurgle and bubble. Barracuda grabs her by the hair and turns her over. She rolls up her sleeves. She gets an old hard brush rich with pine soap. Then she starts scrubbing away.

18

Later. The room has been cleaned. The cat litter and the cats have been removed. There are new curtains up. The sheets have been changed, and there is a pleasant light in the room instead of the dreary one that had been there for months. Barracuda has changed from her clothes upon which Ms. Swille's blood had spattered. Bangalang is on one side, combing Ms. Swille's hair; Barracuda is on the other. They are using long golden combs. Ms. Swille is propped up in the bed. She has a Band-Aid on her skin, here and there. Her skin is a raw red from the scalding hot water. She is drinking a tall glass of milk between sobs.

"Barracuda hates to do what she had to do with her darlin, but her darlin was letting her darlin self go. Barracuda no like that. Barracuda no like. Come from a proud fambly. Good fambly. Remember when you used to help fix waffles for your Daddy and Mr. Jefferson Davis? 'Can I help, Mammy Barracuda?' you used to ax. Bless yo little soul. You'd even carry some out back for Mr. Davis' body servant, Sammy Davis. Round here wearing Levi negligees. No wonder Bossman Swille took to having a separate bedroom. You can't blame the man for wanting to be away from you, the condition you was in.

"It all started that time you came home from Radcliffe. That Yankee school. I told your Daddy that that school wasn't doing nothing but bothering your head, but he wouldn't listen. Then you come home. People glad to see you. Then how you act. How you act! Call them a bunch of antebellum anal retentive assholes. Then we found you reading that book by that old simple Stowe fambly. Old crazy fambly. That wild Harriet one. And her adulteratin brother Henry, ain't got a bit of sense, and her suffragette sister Isabelle—she crazy too. Jesus tired of them. Jesus tired. That's why her son got wounded in the war and the other one drownded. That's Jesus gettin back at them for they lies. And the way she bad-mouth old Simon Legree. He a good man. He always say, 'Now, anything you need, just ask for it, Mammy Barracuda. Just speak up, you can have it.' Lorrrrrd."

Mammy Barracuda is preening and plaiting the Mistress' hair, looking googly-eyed toward the ceiling. She pauses a minute. "You try to raise them and look what they done done. Marry a rich man like that. Arthur Swille III. Anybody else would be proud. Proud. Like a fairy queen in one of them Princess books. Worrying him so. Now I want you to get your basket of violets together, do you hear me?"

"But—"

"Don't choo be buttin me! You gon pick some violets; that is, after you have come down and personally looked after the preparing of the breakfast for the men. Then . . . What else, Bangalang?"

Bangalang picks up an in-Castle memo from the night-stand top. "Then there will be a garden poetry reading of Edgar Poe."

"I think for dat occasion you shall wear a bonnet and a cloak and some jewelry . . . some of dat nice golden jewelry. Maybe your goldbug pin."

"I gave that to Mr. Poe to pawn. He's always seeking 'loans,' as he calls them. Says he can't figure out royalty reports."

"Then after that I want you to come to my office, and I'll

have you fill out the details for the rest of the day, which will include a tea for some of the neighborhood belles, an outdoor cookie sale to help the po 'Federate hospital . . ."

"But, Barracuda, don't you see that that's exploitin—"

"You shush about the 'sploitin.' Now I want you to roll over."

"What are you doing now?"

Barracuda, one eye shut, one eye open, is preparing a long hypodermic needle filled with cc's of Valium.

"What . . . what are you doing, Barracuda?"

"This ain't gon take but a little time. And don't worry, it won't hurt a bit. Just a little pinch."

"But, Barracuda . . ."

"Barracuda wants her darlin to turn over now. Cooperate, I don't have all day. A famous military man is coming for dinner tomorrow, and I have to prepare the menu. Tomorrow night while they're dining I want you to make an appearance. When the men is lighting up the cigars, you will enter the room and make a few courtesies and stay until they have recited the 'Ode to the Southern Belle.' Tomorrow A.M. you will return to watering flowers, selling cookies, fanning yourself, fluttering your eyebrows and blushing at the flirtatious remarks of the Southern gen'mens. I want that drawl back, too. You sound too Yankee, that's part of your problem. But tomorrow you goin to look fine. Like nothing ever happened. You gon look chaste—not too chaste, though, a wee bit coquettish, refined. Now turn over. You will be quality people again and quit yo old tomcat ways. Hrmph! Grumph!"

"But, Barracuda . . ."

Barracuda gives the signal to Bangalang, who grabs one of her Mistress' arms and one leg while Barracuda catches the others. They turn her over. Barracuda squats atop her and slowly gives the injection. Ms. Swille emits a low moan and passes out.

Barracuda turns out the lights.

Ms. Swille comes to, momentarily. "Barracuda, when is my son coming back from Africa?"

Barracuda and Bangalang look at each other.

"He'll be back soon, now you go to sleep."

But Ms. Swille is already asleep, snoring. Barracuda rips out the radio cord. She carries the radio under her arm and walks out of the room, followed by Bangalang, her aide.

Mammy Barracuda stands in the center of the room, her arms folded. She gives orders with her head. Pointing in this direction, that direction. Tapping her foot when annoyed. Giving some eye-dagger when mad. Not smiling but showing a wee twinkle when pleased. Bangalang is second in command, following through, taking inventory of every detail.

Ms. Swille sits in the chair facing the huge mirror. The slave girls and the pickaninnys are applying makeup, combing, brushing, manicuring; others are bringing out the wardrobe, preparing to put Ms. Swille in it. She sits at the dressing table, in her slip.

"I feel like . . . like I'm in a dollhouse."

"Now, don't get smart. We doin this for your own good. You remember what happened the other night when you was acting reckless. Now don't be acting reckless. When we finish with you, you gon put Jeanette MacDonald to shame."

"Yes, Mammy."

"That's mo like it."

Bangalang drops a pincushion. Mammy Barracuda rushes over and shakes her a little. "Be careful with dat. What's wrong wit choo? If you don't shape up, I'm gon take away this good job you got and send you to the fields. You don't want to go to the fields, now do you?"

"No, Mammy Barracuda."

"Who da boss?"

"You are, Mammy Barracuda."

"Who?"

"You."

"Let me hear it from all of you," she said, her hand cupping an ear.

The girls say, "You are, Barracuda. You the boss. Our leader . . ."

"I didn't hear one person say it."

The girls stop. They stare at Ms. Swille.

"Barracuda, please don't . . . don't humiliate me before the girls . . ."

"You've given up your respect. Listening to that old Beecher woman. Talking about taking up whoring . . ."

"Free love, Barracuda. That's different . . ."

"I don't care what you call it, you syphilitic muskrat . . ."

The girls oooo and awwwww.

"Now I give you one more chanct. Who the boss?"

"You are, Barracuda."

The girls giggle. They are standing before the mirror, and Ms. Swille is blushing.

"Don't she look beautiful."

"OOOOOO. So preeeeeety."

"Don't look like the same person, look quality again."

"Look ten years younger."

Mammy Barracuda, lighting up a corncob pipe, makes a twirling motion with her finger. Ms. Swille, holding the hem of her dress, begins to spin about and model as the girls gape and sigh.

"Have yo butt down in the parlor when the gen'men begin to light up their cigars. All right, count off."

Ms. Swille stands in the middle of the room. The other girls stiffen. With her hands behind her back, Barracuda inspects the woman. "Turn around, fool." Barracuda grabs Ms. Swille and spins her around some more. She looks at the woman directly, eye to eye. She looks at the girls, and "marching like a grenadier," she exits from the room. The girls scurry out like the corps de ballet, leaving Ms. Swille alone.

She begins to sob. There is a gust of wind. The kerosene lamps go out. There is a sudden chill in the room.

19

There was a frost on the Lake Erie steamer *The North America.*
Quaw Quaw had gone inside the cabin to read. Raven stood
at the rail gazing out across Lake Erie. The cold air was hitting
him in the face. It felt good, and he was warm in an overcoat
he had just bought with some of the "Flight to Canada"
money; it was made of rare apaupala wool and was bear-brown.
He was thinking about the kind of fashion he'd buy now that
he was becoming a successful anti-slavery lecturer. A man came
up. He had on a vest of "oriental" design. He carried a tall silk
hat. Black kid gloves. He wore a black waistcoat. He carried a
cane whose head was the head of a serpent.

"That's some lake, huh? I've made this trip from Cleveland many times but I still can't get used to its wonder." He
was distinguished-looking.

"Oh, are you commuting to a job in Buffalo?"

"No, not at all," the stranger said. "I have been abroad,
but nothing compares with the serenity of this lake, this peace.
It has a special meaning to me. You see, I used to carry fugitive
slaves to Canada from Cleveland and Buffalo."

"Really," Quickskill said, smiling.

"Those were the days, back in the forties. We used to get
into some pretty tough scrapes with the claimants and coadju-

tors. They'd be watching the steamers for their goods. They
were a pretty ignorant bunch, though. Sometimes we'd disguise the male slaves as women, and the female slaves as men,
and they'd walk right past the suckers! Ha!"

"They were that dumb, huh? You must have had some
pretty trying moments though."

"We did. Once we had a run-in with a slave trader named
Bacon Tate. He was after a couple named Standford who were
living in Saint Catherine's, Ontario, a delightful place. Well,
he sent in some thugs to take them, and they were heading
back across the Black Rock Ferry to the U.S. when me and
some friends heard about it. We caught up with them and
freed the Standfords. Well, old man Tate went and got the
law, and before we got them on the boat, they caught up with
us. Well, man, you should have seen the fight. Pistols going off.
People clubbing each other. During the melee the Standfords
escaped on the ferry. Ha! Never will forget that."

"Those must have been exciting times."

"Yeah, they were all right." There is a far-off gaze in his
brown eyes. "Where you heading?"

"Canada."

"Vacation?"

"No, I'm escaping. I've booked passage on this steamer
under a pseudonym. My master is after me."

"You have to be kidding me, stranger. The war is over."

"You don't know my Master. He views me as something
that belongs to him. The laws which apply to other slavemasters don't apply to him. He's the slavemasters' slavemaster."

"A real case, huh?"

"You can say that again."

"Well, if I can be of any help, contact my agent. Here's
my card."

It read *William Wells Brown, Anti-Slavery Lecturer,
Writer.*

"William Wells Brown. *The* William Wells Brown?"

"Can't be two of us, Mr. . . . Mr. . . ."

"Quickskill."

"Mr. Quickskill. What line of work are you in?"

"Why, I guess you might call me an anti-slavery writer, too, but I . . . well in comparison with your reputation, I . . . I'm just a beginner. I read your novel *Clotel* and . . . I just want to say, Mr. Brown, that you're the greatest satirist of these times."

"Why, thank you, Mr. Quickskill. I'm glad you like my books. What kind of stuff do you write?"

"I . . . well, my poem 'Flight to Canada' is going to be published in *Beulahland Review*. It kind of imitates your style, though I'm sure the critics are going to give me some kind of white master. A white man. They'll say that he gave me the inspiration and that I modeled it after him. But I had you in mind . . . Mr. Brown, I don't want to take up any of your time, but would you like to see one of my poems?"

Brown smiled broadly. "I'd love to, lad. Do you have it with you?"

"It's in my cabin. I'll be right back."

Quickskill ran to the cabin, almost knocking down one of the lakers, he was so excited. He dashed inside. "Quaw Quaw! Quaw Quaw! William Wells Brown—" She was lying on the bed, sobbing. He reached for her arm.

"Don't you touch me. Leave me alone. I was tired of reading Dickens and so I took your manuscript out of the suitcase. I read the poem. Why didn't you tell me? Why didn't anyone?"

"You loved him so, Quaw Quaw. I didn't want to be the one. I don't need to knock another man to gain a woman."

"But . . . I've been with this man since I was fourteen. He raised me. Sent me to school. Paid my bills. I loved him. But if I had known . . ." She breaks into sobs, burying her head in the wet pillow.

Quickskill walked over to the dresser where the poem lay. He didn't want her to learn about it this way. No, not this way.

The Saga of Third World Belle

Third World Belle
My Indian Princess
No one has the heart to tell
You, so I will

Your favorite pirate uses
Your Dad's great-chief's skull
As an ashtray
And sold your Mom's hand-knitted
Robes to Buffalo Bill's
Wild West Show

He buried your brother alive
In a sealed-off section of the
Metropolitan Museum

To you he's a "heavy" aesthete
Born in '27
While I am a native mind riding
Bareback, backwards through
a wood of words and when I stumble
I get my Ibo* up and hobble
like a bloody-footed slave
Traveling from Virginia to

*Ibos: a fiercely proud African tribe who'd rather cut their throats than be sold into slavery.

Ohio and if I stumble again
I get my Cherokee up and smell
My way to the clearing

Your Apache temper snaps at me
Even before I open my trap

But I still love you my
Mountain-climbing woman with
A rope all around your waist
My rider of Killer Whales

I'm on a fox hunt for you baby
Got my black cap and red coat on
I'm on a fox hunt for you baby
Got my black cap and red coat on

Just like a coyote cassetting amorous
Howls
In Sugar Blues

I airmail them to you
In packages of Hopi Dolls

Ah ouoooooo! Ah ouoooooo!

20

Mooootttthhhhheeeeerrrrr. Mooooottttthhhhheeeeerrrr.

"What can that be?" Ms. Swille said at the dresser, turning her head around.

Moooooottttttthhhhhheeeeeeerrrrrr.

Then she saw a foot—no, not really a foot but some strange reticulated claw—entering the room from the wall opposite her. And then a clammy-looking hand . . . well, not exactly a hand. It was a human figure, but not exactly; the skin belonged to that of a crocodile, but the head—oh no—the head, it was Mitchell's head. Mitchell, the anthropologist; it was his head.

"Mitchell, you're supposed to be in the Congo. What on earth are you doing in that outfit?"

"I hate to greet you in this awful state, Mother, but, well, you see, I was killed."

"Killed! My son! You were . . . they told me that you had extended your stay in the Congo. Killed!" She begins to sob.

"I know, Mom," the creature says, now having moved to next to where she's seated in front of the mirror. "They never tell you anything. But my body was never found. The Snake Society was mean, and they, well, they have some strange ideas about the supernatural. You don't hear them longing for 'heb-

bin,' as the kinks call it here. They threw me to this crocodile
called Aldo. He ate everything but my head . . . He . . ."

"Oh, oh, oh! No! Please, Mitchell, they didn't."

"You can't blame them, Mom. They condemned me to
go about in this outfit for eternity. It's cold where I am. A
cold-blooded place, as they say in Sacramento. The other side.
Boy, are the smokes going to be in for a surprise. I had to tell
you this, Mother; I know that even the little picks who remove
the worms from the tobacco know more about what's going on
here than you do. The smokes do the same thing there that
they do here, only overtime. The unglorious occupations. You
see, they found out that I wasn't really on an anthropology
expedition but was checking things for Dad. Your husband, my
father, is one macabre fiend. No wonder he has Poe down here
all the time. Do you know what he did?"

"What did he do, son?"

"Sent my head to the National Archives and took it off
his taxes."

"Oh, son, did he do that?"

"I didn't want to meddle in the internal affairs of the
Congo. He had me spending my time making resources maps.
All I wanted to do was bring back some shrunken heads for my
museum collection. You know, the one uptown that Dad gave
me."

"I'm furious. Son, do you see me shaking? Do you see
what a terrible state I'm in? That smoke, Mammy Barracuda,
just makes my life miserable. I have no authority any more, and
when I do exercise my functions she says things like 'Dit out
of my way,' or 'Dit out of my kitchen.' She has some strange
hold on Master Swille."

"That's not all, Mother. He has this film library. When
his friends were riding high before the war, he'd invite them
up here. He showed terrible pictures of slaves being tortured
and killed. Close-ups of them biting each other's ears off. His
friends would watch this, drink Tennessee whiskey and eat box
lunches. It was awful."

"No, no, spare me."

"And not only that. He flogged Queen Victoria. Yet she refused to give him a title."

"What!"

"That's when you were away in New York on behalf of one of the Beecher causes. He was in England on business. Queen Victoria and Prince Albert visited Dad for the purpose of his loaning England some money so that they could buy Burma. Well, Barracuda found a copy of *Uncle Tom's Cabin* in her room, and Dad had her fettered before the whole establishment. Others say that the Queen refused him a barony. And Mom, Dad's gotten mixed up with this Lord Gladstone who's a friend of Marquis de Sade who is introducing some new pastime for the rich called Sadism."

"What on earth is that, son?"

"Something to do with whips. But sometimes screws. Sadists have closets full of lashes. They trade fettering devices."

"But we do that all the time down here, son."

"That's why Gladstone came out for the Confederacy."

"Why . . . I don't follow."

"Gladstone is a leading Sadist. He's into flagellation. He . . . he whips himself, Mother, tortures and beats himself."

"Oh my God, you mean your father is mixed up with that outfit?"

"Yes, Mother. They want to make the South into their headquarters so that all of their followers can come here and practice their ways without being persecuted. They've referred to Virginia as the Sadist's Canada. Well, they had the Queen of England whipped, Mother. The Sadists have about captured the Crown. They're all over the world, whipping people in the name of England. Whipping. Screaming. Beating people for the Queen."

"Zounds! What horrors!"

"Victoria's old whale-white skin started spotting red. Then they blotched her, wringed her. And they stretched her. And Prince Albert stood there real dignified, Mother. Real dignified. And under so much stress. And speaking of stress,

Mother, they brought in that stud, Big Jim. Mother, you know the one who goes about saying motherfuck a motherfucker all the time. Then it got kinky, Mom. Real kinky. They really needed that loan bad, but Dad didn't get the barony. He's now trying to get a circle of corrupt lords to persuade the Queen to bestow one upon him. He's a saber-toothed guppy, Mom. Look at me. I have to go through eternity this way. You know, it's hard to get crocodile skin clean, real hard. Dirt digs deep in the scales. I can't control the tail. All I wanted to do was hunt some heads for my museum collection. Now look . . . I talk in this evil nasal twang."

"Oh, son. I know what to do," she said as the specter crept back through the wall.

Outside a thunderstorm began. It was thrashing across the sky. She thought she heard someone calling. A familiar voice. Echoing across the meadows. A sweet soprano voice.

21

At one end of the table, the top of which bore three white candles and a basket of fruit and flowers, sat, dining, Arthur Swille. At the other, a man dressed in a Union military uniform. He was much decorated. His chest looked like a medal bed.

". . . then Mudd took the wounded man in and bandaged him. Everything is proceeding according to plan."

"Good. So no one can trace it to me?"

"We made sure of that. One of our men, posing as a marshal, shot him to death as he was running out of the barn. The newspapers are getting suspicious. You know, the story we put out that all the conspirators burned up in the fire."

"Whitewash."

"Nothing about whitewash. Just suspicious. We did it away from the TV cameras. Told the video people that we couldn't guarantee their safety."

"What about the woman who ran the inn?"

"Oh, she doesn't know anything about you."

"Good job, General. When do you think you can get Johnson down here to see me? The great Plebeian."

"Ha ha. That was some speech he made at Abe's second inauguration, huh?" He swallowed two tumblers of whiskey

before he went on. "Lincoln was so mad. You should have seen
Abe. He said if we allowed that son of a bitch to say another
word, he'd fire the whole cabinet. Johnson's having d.t.'s now.
Says he sees Lincoln's ghost. We have to get Jacobson to give
him injections. They're beginning to whisper in the Capitol.
You know how the town talks. We listened in on one of
Anderson's lines, and he's thinking about doing a column on
it. The man has no class. The rude Tennessean. Got into a
fistfight with a heckler."

"He what?"

"Wrestling in the streets with a buckrah. You know, Abe
had his bad points, but Abe was cold. These fancy Confederates were trying to arrange a peace deal. We were all sitting
on *The River Queen.* And one of them cited Charles I for some
precedent. Some action Charles I took. They wanted to win a
few points. Well, Abe . . . Abe started to clutch his lapels with
his fingers. And he leaned back until his eyes were focused on
the ceiling. And he kinda got that twinkle in his eyes that
brought lines in their corners closer together. And he said, 'All
I know about Charles I is that he went and got himself be-
headed.' You know, the South will never forgive him for declar-
ing medical supplies contraband at Richmond."

"Look, General, I didn't mind Lincoln. Had him down
here." Swille stops and begins munching on apple pie.
"Hmmmmm. This is delicious. Pompey . . ." addressing the
small slave standing against the wall, "go and have them order
Mammy Barracuda a ruby ring from Cartier's. Anyway, as I
was saying, I liked the man. But he gave away all that property.
All that property. Gave away other people's property. Why, I
tried to loan him the money to buy the slaves. What made him
change his mind, General?"

The general puts down a wineglass. "Toward the end he
kept having visions of himself as a statue. Sitting in the chair
and staring out over the Potomac. He started to believe it. He
began to see himself as a great Emancipator, Mr. Swille. Got
hooked by his own line. Then he saw visions of himself lying
in state on the catafalque in the Capitol rotunda. I finally

realized why Abe was an infidel, Massa Swille."

"Why's that, General?" Swille says, sipping a cup of coffee.

"He couldn't imagine anybody being Christ but him. He could never deal with the infidel issue they kept raising in his campaigns about our Lord being the real Christ."

The Military Man reaches over and carves some salmon, which rests in a china platter, an idiot look on its face, surrounded by sliced lemons.

"Strange times, don't you think, General? What happens to such people in these times? I think Abe must have gotten nigger fever."

"What's that, Mr. Swille?"

"Nigger fever. Niggers do something to you. I've seen white people act strange under their influence. First you dream about niggers, little niggers mostly; little niggers, sitting eating watermelons, grinning at you. Then you start dreaming about big niggers. Big, big niggers. Big, big niggers walking all on top of you; then you got niggers all over you, then they got you. Now they got white men fighting white men on land taken away from the Indians—Rappahannock, Chattanooga. It's spooky. As long as they're in this country, this country is under their spell. It'll be one great HooDoo sea."

"I understand the wisdom of your decision, Mr. Swille."

"Would you like some dessert?"

"No, thank you, Mr. Swille, think I'll just sit here, light up a cigar and relax next to this wonderful fireplace."

"Had it shipped over here from Windsor Castle. The Duke was glad to get the money, too. Glad to. Went out and gave away his food stamps."

"You spend a lot of time over there, don't you, Mr. Swille?"

"That I do, General. Though my body inhabits the Swille Castle, my mind is in Europe. What's that you always say, Uncle Robin?"

"Say what, Massa Swille?"

"What's that old colored saying?"

"Oh, you mean, you can take my body but not my soul?"

"That's the one. Americans, both North and South, hate the slaves, and they're slaves themselves. If we didn't have the cocoas, we'd get the Irish. Did you hear the one about the Irish map? Shows you where the roads don't go. Get it? Shows you where the roads don't go."

"Sir, I've never heard it put so sanguinely. Sir, you . . . you should run things yourself instead of hiring people, sir. You should . . ."

Swille, now leaning back, flicking ashes from his Havanna into an ashtray, says, "I know. I know. Uncle Robin asked me the same thing. But the Family would get mad. It would be an embarrassment to the Family."

"Incidentally, speaking of the Family, how's the crocodile-killing coming on?"

"We brought in the army corps of engineers. Some congressman from Lawrence, Kansas, some kind of offbeat town, objected and called it genocide. I'd like to parachute feetfirst into Lawrence and clean it up, that anti-slavery hotbed."

"Why can't you do something about that town?"

Ms. Swille enters the room. Uncle Robin starts. Swille and the general rise. She is decked out in finery—hoop skirt, Paris shoes, hair in belle curls. She is thin as Twiggy and wan as Morris' Guenevere; titties the size of spuds. Swille and the general lift their wineglasses.

"How's about a toast to Southern womanhood," the general says.

"I don't want your toasts. You Swille swine."

She moves into the room, and from her handbag she pulls a Stonewall Jackson rocket-powered miniature cannon, leave a hole in a man the size of an eightball.

"Dear, what's come over you?" Swille says, dropping his glass, rolling his eyes about like Mantan Mooreland in the Charlie Chan movies.

"My son. You killed my son. All he wanted to do was hunt some shrunken heads for his museum, and you had him over there . . . you disgusting . . ."

"Look, dear, he asked me if there was anything he could do for me in the Congo. I didn't think it'd hurt for him to look in on some copper. Just think, all the copper, Mother, radiant . . . yellow!"

"You Moloch! You Mammon! You . . . you Beelzebub! Oh, this man, my husband," she said, turning to the Military Man.

The Military Man nodded nervously, clutching his white linen napkin in his hand.

"You have to forgive her, General. She's, well . . . she's suffering from melancholy. It's induced by the miasma in our atmosphere."

"Yes, that's it. Try to change the subject. There you go. You're always changing the subject on me, treating me like the field help around here. As though I came with the land, like arrangements in the feudal ages. Military Man," she says, "he has a mammy who says abrasive things to me, and she manhandles me and confiscates my belongings. And he has concubines. The slave girls walk around with all of my jewelry on. Oh, the decadence. Tell them about the decadence down here, Military Man. The great immoral decadence. Tell them in the land beyond the screams."

She gags as if to bring up phlegm in her throat. "And his concubines. Why, some of the girls are mere babies. And if that's not enough, he belongs to this awful Magnolia Baths. He stays there for weeks sometimes, and when he returns, his lips are pudgy and there's a steady string of saliva hanging from his bottom lip, and his fingers look . . . look gross, and he sits there for weeks staring at the wall. I think he must be on belladonna. Have you noticed his eyes?"

She's focused her attention on Swille and hasn't noticed until now that the Military Man has left through the side door. "Well, haven't you noticed, Robin?"

"Now, Ms. Swille, I want you to leave me out of the argument you and Mr. Swille is having. It ain't right for the slave to tell the Master and the Missus how to conduct their affairs."

"True, Robin. You're such a wise man."

"Thank you, Ms. Swille."

"He should have set you free by now . . . Oh, he's such a suave Swille swine!"

"But, dear—" Swille says, moving toward her.

"You keep away from me."

She is now holding the gun with two trembling hands. Swille continues to move toward her away from the fireplace in which every log is afire and heating the entire room.

"I've been watching you . . . A . . ."

"You see, it's been so long, you've forgotten my name. It's Arthur Swille. Don't you remember?"

"Of course I remember. How can I forget that when we were six years old my father and your father made our betrothal. And the letters I wrote to you when I was in Europe. Remember those letters? The tormented sad letters I wrote you from the cafés. The telegrams of pathos. The palliative and passionate night letters. You remember the letters, Arthur?"

"Yes. And our wedding. Why, all of Richmond must have been there." Swille is near to where she is standing. "But now you're even more beautiful."

"You mean you like my white tongue and my sallow looks."

"Of course, my dear."

"And my bones protruding, my legs and my ribs showing."

"It's so . . . so aesthetic, dear."

"And you like the way I've become so delicate that I won't go out of doors for fear the sun will melt me or that I will stumble in a puddle and drown or if somebody said boo I'd keel over?"

"You're lovely, my dear."

She lays down the pistol and rushes into his arms. He embraces her. A gust of wind opens the door. The candles go out.

"Uncle Robin, would you go downstairs and fetch some more candles?"

Uncle Robin leaves the room in which Ms. Swille is sobbing against her husband's chest, the pistol lying on the table.

"Now there, dear," Swille said, comforting her.

"I wasn't boycotting, I wanted you to notice me. You weren't paying attention to me."

"I'll make up for that, dear. We'll have parties again. Why, Eddie Poe told me he had some opiates that were so good that you contemplated the world in a book's binding for one whole day. We can travel—Majorca, the Greek Islands—you name it."

"Oh, Arthur, Arthur, I knew I was doing the right thing, becoming like her. That's what you wanted, wasn't it, Arthur? I've become just like her . . ."

"I don't follow you, dear—"

Just then there was a giggle—a shrill giggle, arising from some remote decaying city, deep under and far away.

"Don't listen to him. He'll never love you. He'll never love anyone but me."

"Vivian," shrieked Ms. Swille and folded like a bag into her husband's arms.

"What . . . what are you doing here? Go back . . ." gasped Swille.

"You know you don't love her. You'll never give up your licentious Hedonist Award of 1850, the Golden Dawn Club, the Epicurean Club and the Bohemian Club. You'll never give up me, will you, brother? Out in my sepulcher by the sea. By the grey dismal seaaaaa," she said, a hideous sardonic grin on her face.

"Get back," Swille cries moving back from his sister, who is approaching him, a filmy scarf, white-death negligee, feet white and ashen, carrying some strange book of obscure lore. It is leather-bound, wearing its words embossed in gold.

"At first I thought the notion was disgusting, abominable even. You was violatin' . . . my chaste Southern belle upbringing out there in my tomb, standing over the coffin lid, real hard like that. You put my hand on it and made me feel it." Her evil green eyes are staring at him, her body a silhouette under her ragged white gown, her long fingernails dripping blood. Her wildcat hair. Her sinister, diabolical face.

"No, please—"

"And then there under the moonlight you slid the lid back altogether and then you climbed in . . . and each night after that, you'd hold on to me, cling to me, there in the silence of the cemetery. And you would become so peaceful . . . so peaceful. And you said I was your fair lady and you were my knight and we were married in Death . . . Please—"

She grabs her brother and then is all atop him. He falls against the fireplace, and she is laughing, staring into his eyes from her gaping skeleton sockets. Fighting and screaming, Swille backs into the fire. Fire grabs his coattails. Fire is hungry. Fire eats.

When Robin returned with the candles, he was shocked at the hideous scene before him. Swille was crackling and bouncing from the fire. Ms. Swille had been flung across the room. Robin rushed over and lifted her by the arms. He dragged her out into the hall, where Pompey stood in vigil.

"Pompey! Something awful has happened! Massa Swille is on fire."

"Yeah," Pompey said, standing next to a vase in his green silk dress coat, wearing his white-powdered wig. "I figured something was up when I saw that general hightailing it out of here and I heard all of that screaming."

"Well, you try to revive Ms. Swille, while I run and fetch some water for Massa Swille."

"Good idea," Pompey said. "If the man's afire, you should get some water. Maybe that will help," Pompey said as he began to slap Ms. Swille.

Robin walks to the elevator. Waits for it. It goes down to the basement, then begins to rise to the third floor while Robin waits. He presses the button again and hears popping sounds coming from the dining room, followed by Ms. Swille's screams. She is coming around. Pompey shrugs his shoulders and glances Robin's way. Robin stands at the elevator, and this time the elevator goes to the top of the roof and then suddenly drops to the basement.

He decides to take the steps and starts down. He reaches the kitchen and runs to the sink. He begins to draw a bucket of water. Bangalang appears.

"Something terrible has happened, Bangalang. Mr. Swille has been pushed into the flames."

"Did she kill him?" Bangalang asks.

"He's not dead yet, he's on fire."

Bangalang goes to the faucet and turns off the water.

"Bangalang, what's the matter with you, turning off the water?"

"I was just trying to help. Mammy Barracuda says when you turn the faucet on, you're not suppose to forget to turn it off."

Robin, having filled the bucket, begins to return to the dining room. She catches his arm, "Robin, when you going to take me out, like you said you were going to? On one of those trips you make for Mr. Swille."

"Shut up, girl. You want to get me into trouble? You young wimmen all alike. No discretion." He leaves a giggling Bangalang behind.

When Robin returned to the dining room it was too late. The fire was sleeping off its dinner.

Part III
THE BURNING
OF RICHMOND

What are we all—white Negroes, or serfs or what? What is the little man, Jeff Davis? Where did he get it? Is this man one of the Caesars? Or is he one of the Medici? Or perhaps the last of the Bothic . . .? Or is he veritably "the last of the Bourbons"? Can it be so? Or is he indeed that little backwoods man from Mississippi . . . the very worst executive officer known in the modern world since the time of his prototype, James II of England.

The Charleston Mercury
February 7, 1865

22

What the American Arthurians couldn't win on the battlefield will now be fought out on the poetry field. Lincoln, the Saxon chief, is slain. Lincoln, London, two towns in Britain—Lincoln, London, England, Lincoln London England—the savage sounds of rock worshipers. "Anglo-Saxon was abandoned to the use of rustics and hinds, who knew no other," Sir Walter Scott said. Sir Scott.

Old man Ruffin, who fired the first shot against the Union at Fort Sumter, shot himself when he heard that Lee had surrendered.

Jefferson Davis is captured, disguised in his wife's hoops, shawl and rainproof coat. Davis' defenders say it's a lie. Historians still debate this.

Oscar Wilde, "The Great Decadent," would say, "His fall after such an able and gallant pleading in his own cause must necessarily arouse pity." Davis later invited "The Apostle of Aesthetics" to his Mississippi homestead, where Wilde "charmed" the ladies. Maybe it was Wilde's knee breeches and the sunflower pinned to the lapel of his coat that appealed to them. Raised by mammies, the South is dandyish, foppish, pimpish; its writers are Scott, Poe, Wilde, Tennyson; its assassin left behind a trunk in which was found: "clothes in fine silk velvets; silks, ermine and crimson; and also hats, caps, plumes, boots, shoes, etc."

Davis later said that he desired to carry on guerrilla warfare in the hills of Virginia. Davis missed the point. Davis, who was accused by *The Charleston Mercury* of treating Southerners like "white Negroes," misread his people. It wasn't the idea of winning that appealed to them. It was the idea of being ravished. Decadent and Victorian writing both use the romantic theme of fair youth slumbering. Fair youth daydreaming. Fair youth struck down. In the New Orleans Mardi Gras, that great Confederate pageant, the cult of Endymion has a whole evening. Saturday.

Davis claims he tried to wrestle his captors to the ground from their horses. He is a proud patrician with a "chiseled" nose and tells the Union soldier to kindly take his "buckrah" hands off of him. The rude Yankee soldiers refer to him as "Jeff," and when he is jailed they draw cartoons of him hanging from a tree on the wall of his cell.

23

Buffalo, New York. The reading was held by the Anti-Slavery Society of Western New York at the Eagle Tavern, located at Main and Court streets. Above the entrance was an eagle holding in its talons a banner which read, "Our Rights, Our Liberty." It was a red building, three stories high, with a balustrade fronting the roof.

There was a spacious entrance hall and a reception parlor. On one side was a bar. Inside the bar was a wood-and-charcoal fireplace. On the walls there were photos and autographs of famous customers: Dan Webster, General Lafayette.

Before the reading they had dined on roasted and fricasseed fowl, boiled potatoes and vegetables.

For cocktails, Quaw Quaw, Quickskill and their hosts had partaken of a large decanter of brandy. Their hosts were very friendly and had arranged for them to be taken to Canada by a Friend. The reading, however, was far from successful.

Things kept going wrong with the microphone. The lights went out a couple of times. When Quickskill mentioned, in passing, that Millard Fillmore, a well-known Buffalo man and first chancellor of the University of Buffalo, had signed the Fugitive Slave Law, one heckler threw a tomato; the heckler was hustled out, but Quickskill's lecture suit got smeared, and some got in his hair. He had had it done in the style of Frederick Douglass and Abe Lincoln and John Wilkes Booth, one side of the forehead shaved back V-like. Some of the people in the front row began to snore, and the black help from the kitchen stood on the side, making comments, talking loud and staring at him evilly.

He wasn't a performer, and some of the people in the audience wanted more fire. He remembered the man at Lincoln University who said, "Quickskill, you all right. You make some good points. But you ought to put a little more fire into it." And when he said "fire," he hit his left open palm with his right fist. A little more fire. They wanted to get warm.

Sometimes he felt like a cheap Sears, Roebuck furnace. A little fire, but not enough to heat the whole house. Some of the other slaves were downright rude. They came in late, and when they didn't like what he was saying, got up, making comments, and walked out. Other slaves, however, sat at attention. They'd begun some kind of Raven cult. He didn't want to have a cult. A Raven is always on the move. A cult would tie him down.

Not only were the slaves enslaved by others, but they often, in subtle ways, enslaved each other. As soon as he and Quaw Quaw had entered the tavern, two of the female slave help had begun to let out their ignorant slave cackle, giving them signifying looks.

Slaves judged other slaves like the auctioneer and his clients judged them. Was there no end to slavery? Was a slave condemned to serve another Master as soon as he got rid of one? Were overseers to be replaced by new overseers? Was this some game, some fickle punishment for sins committed in former lives? Slavery on top of slavery? Would he ever be free to do what he pleased as long as he didn't interfere with another man's rights? Slaves held each other in bondage; a hostile stare from one slave criticizing the behavior of another slave could be just as painful as a spiked collar—a gesture as fettering as a cage.

Some of the people had remained behind to chat with Quickskill about his work, including the two Friends who were his hosts. They were eating Freedom Hamburgers. A little

Union flag hung from the toothpick that went through the buns and the meat. Quaw Quaw was still upset by the poem. Once in a while he would squeeze her hand. She'd lay her head on his shoulder. He wondered if they'd ever be as deeply in love with each other as before. Would it be a "cerebral" relationship, with them occasionally fucking like crazy animals? They said they wouldn't become involved the way they had before. They'd just enjoy each other, learn from each other. She was a twentieth-century woman. Way ahead of the Beecherites. Finally a man appeared at the door. The two Friends nodded.

Quickskill and Quaw Quaw picked up their baggage and followed the man who was standing in the doorway. He said, "The carriage that will take you to Black Rock has arrived. Good luck, my brother, my sister."

They got in. This was it. There was a Ryder moon over the water when they arrived at the ferry. They could see the yacht not far from the shore. The yacht that would take them to freedom.

A man rowed them out in a canoe. "I thought we'd stopped these runs since the war was over. What's going on?"

"My slavemaster, Arthur Swille. You don't understand. These issues don't apply to him. He sees me as his chattel, and he won't rest until he recovers me. If I'd taken Greyhound or Air Canada, his men would have seized me at the terminal."

"Some kind of maniac."

"You might say that."

They had reached the boat. The man who'd rowed them delivered them over to another man who helped them onto the boat. Already Quickskill's heart was pounding. Quaw Quaw was pleased, too. This was an "adventure" for her. They were directed to a room where they would greet their benefactor, who must have been pretty wealthy, because the yacht was a luxurious boat. They opened the door of the room they were directed to. He saw the man. Quaw Quaw had a shocked look on her face.

"Hey, you ain't no Quaker," Quickskill said, for it was her husband, Yankee Jack.

He was wearing a pin-striped Savile Row suit. Cuff links

from Jolly & Rogers. He was wearing a black glove over an artificial hand. He was twirling a fountain pen in his fingers. On the wall was the photo of some kind of swami.

"Well, what do we have here?" The silver earring on his left earlobe glistened. He wore a headrag with a design of a Confederate flag.

Quaw Quaw noticed the ashtray. "That ashtray, Jack, where did you get that ashtray?"

"What ashtray?"

"That one," she said, pointing to the skull which had been polished until it had the appearance of china.

"One of our many . . . well, in the old days when we were still in that crude business, I'm not exactly proud of that . . . I was in my pre-Zen period . . ."

"That's my father, you shit. You killed my father and are now using him as an ashtray. And my brother, you . . ." She went to where the skull rested and began hugging it. "Daddy, Daddy," she said.

"You don't belong to the human race, Yankee Jack, you . . . you pirate," Quickskill stormed. "But you're more suave, more sophisticated than the Gilbert and Sullivan variety. That was a good idea to bring in poets to give you an artsy-craftsy front. You call yourself a 'distributor,' attempting to make yourself respectable. You decide which books, films, even what kind of cheese, no less, will reach the market. At least we fuges know we're slaves, constantly hunted, but you enslave everybody. Making saps of them all. You, the man behind a distribution network, remaining invisible while your underlings become the fall guys. Taking the rap, their reputations capsizing while yours remains afloat. And what you've done to Quaw Quaw, you . . . I have a good mind to—"

Quaw Quaw is really sobbing now.

"Hold on, whatever you are," said Jack. "You know it's not even been determined whether you're a human being. I pay my taxes. Contribute to the March of Dimes. Someone has to get the goods to the market. I'm just a middle man."

"Yeah, a middle man. Cool. Like a model stepping out of

the pages of *The New Yorker* magazine. Scrupulous, precise, correct, but entirely devoid of human feeling."

(A little origin here. Tralaralara was an Indian princess. She was carried off by Yankee Jack. It wasn't just the turquoise beads, the rugs he was after. Nor did he want to corner the Arizona Highways Market. The pirate needed to get through the chief's village to reach the oil before his competitors. His tankers were being out-highwayed. He needed the chief's village out of the way. The chief stood fast and was about to defeat the pirate when someone, an informant, gave away the weaknesses in the chief's defenses. He was taken by Quaw Quaw, a mere fourteen then. He carried her off, and he raised her. Sent her to the best Eastern schools and trained her in "the finer things of life." She is under a white spell and has no feeling for her own people's culture. She does ethnic dances because that's what the colleges want, and she can earn a little extra money and, therefore, be not so dependent upon the pirate's support.)

"You killed my father. How could you? Why didn't you ever tell me?"

"What are you complaining about? Before I raided your village, the chief ran it. Men. Isn't that what you and your suffragette ideas are supposed to be about? That women should have equal power with men? Well, that's what I brought to your people. You should be pleased with your emancipator. I was your people's Lincoln. Not only that, we gave you women absolute power. The freedom to adopt Christian names. We gave you the property. We killed the chiefs and made your medicine men into clowns. Your father got in the way. He had to be . . . removed. And now he's been put to good use. An ashtray. A fitting memorial for a hothead. And we gave your tribe a settlement for that highway we got through. Supplied them with plenty of whiskey. They like whiskey. Lots of money. I thought you didn't identify with any group. Besides, you're doing okay. You don't have to do anything but dance. Dabble in art. I pay all the bills.

"You wanted to be a flower girl? Who do you think paid for that? The bills I got from International Florists! Do you think the honorariums from your ethnic dances paid for that? Look, I'll let you in on a little secret. Do you think that those little colleges paid for your honorariums? No, my foundation supplied them with matching grants. That's how they were able to pay your expenses and your travel. Crying over a fucking skull. As for your mother, she never says anything, and you see her as merely a remnant of the past, but that old lady's got balls. She's the one who gave your father's position away in exchange for a cut of the settlement I made with your people. I'm distributing those robes for her. Got Buffalo Bill to buy some. He deals with her exclusively. She gets forty percent."

"You're a liar," Quaw Quaw says, balling her fists.

"A liar, huh? Okay, take a look at this." He reached into a drawer and handed her what looked like a contract with her mother's signature on it. "I represent her in blankets, beads, rugs. How do you think she bought that Rolls Royce and that house in Santa Cruz, by the ocean? You never questioned it. As long as you were able to spend your winters in Rome and New York, your summers in Taos, you didn't care who was paying for it. There was always plenty. And now that slaves are big in the papers, you went and took one, for diversion. Adventure. And those chapbooks you bought and those bum Bohemian friends of yours, those . . . those 'Franklins'!"

"Those are my friends, they're very talent—"

"Ha. That's a laugh. Me and my friend Leo, the art dealer, were at a party, and one minute this painter friend of yours was pissing in the hostess' fireplace, you know, showing his ass to the bourgeoisie, and next thing you know, when all of the guests weren't looking, he was just about on his hands and knees asking Leo to give him a show. Made all kinds of obscene proposals. Then after the bum left, Leo turns to me and he says, Leo says, 'You see that? They get all denimed and pure downtown, but as soon as they see me, you've never seen such obscene hustling.' Sometimes Leo wishes he'd gone into the garment business."

Quaw Quaw was choking. "You . . . you savage. My father was a great chief. A warrior. My brother was a noble prophet.

None of your gentleman's clothing, your sweet talk, your trucks and planes will hide your savagery."

"The difference between a savage and a civilized man is determined by who has the power. Right now I'm running things. Maybe one day you and Raven will be running it. But for now I'm the one who determines whether one is civilized or savage."

"Let's leave, Quickskill," she said, taking hold of the fugitive slave's hand.

He shook his head. "I didn't come all this way to turn back, Quaw Quaw. 'Once you start out for a place, there's no turning back' is an old HooDoo saying. I mean, Quaw Quaw, I've been looking forward to this all my life. Ever since I was a kid, the old people talked about Canada. I have to have my Canada. Quaw Quaw, I'm going to go if it means swimming across," he said, pointing in the direction of the lights of Niagara Falls, Ontario, across the Niagara.

"All right," Quaw Quaw said. "I'll come too."

Jack laughs. "Okay, go with him. Be pursued by nigger-breakers, 'paddies,' Hays and Allen bloodhounds. Do you know that bloodhounds bite? They can eat five or six pounds of meat per day, and they're not too particular about where it comes from, either. The woods are full of alligators and rattlesnakes. Panthers. That's how your life will be. Afraid of the cop who stops you for speeding or running an intersection. Hiding in the bushes, depressed when the sky is overcast and you can't see the North Star. Somebody always on your tail, and you know, Quaw Quaw, it's hard to tell what you are."

Quaw Quaw removes her hand from Quickskill's and moves back a few bewildered steps.

"You've always complained about your lack of identity." Jack goes on. "What do you think life with him will be like? They'd mistake you for a Negress of hazy origin. You'd have to scrub floors to keep him out of chains."

"Stop," Quaw Quaw says, placing her hands over her ears.

"Do you think it'll be any different in Canada? The free population is getting too big. There have been incidents. Grave incidents. Students from the West Indies manhandled. Fugitives stoned. Canadian parents refusing to send their children to school with 'coloreds.' And have you ever heard of the Mounted Police? Vicious. After those huskies, you'd welcome the bloodhounds. Like wolves. They catch the flesh and won't let go. They have mean habits. And don't let the Prime Minister fool you. He may throw a Potlatch once in a while, but he's still a white man. He sees himself as a white man in a white man's country."

"Race," Quaw Quaw said. "Always race. You and Quickskill always boxing yourself in. What does race have to do with it? People are people."

"Don't listen to him, Quaw Quaw," Raven cried. "Pirates have always undercut our dreams. Canada is beautiful. I hear that on some of the Canadian freeways trucks aren't even allowed."

Quaw Quaw walked to the table. She poured herself a glass of red wine.

Quickskill turned to Jack. "You try to worm your way out of all situations with your forked tongue. You and your graphs and your video charts that show your inventory immediately. It's *unearthly*, the way you hold sway over the American sensibility. They see, read and listen to what you want them to read, see and listen to. You decide the top forty, the best-seller list and the Academy Awards. Breaking the legs of your rivals, making them offers they can't refuse. Yes, you've moved up from looking for buried treasure of dubious value, Yankee Jack. Though I'm a fugitive slave, I'm still a better man than you. The hardships I've had to overcome. My mother sold down the river. My father broken for spitting into the overseer's face. The whippings, the floggings."

"That's not what the revisionists are saying. Don't forget, I read the *New Republic.*"

"Revisionists. Quantitative historians. What does a computer know? Can a computer feel? Make love? Can a computer feel passion?" Quickskill tears off his shirt. "Look at those scars. Look at them! All you see is their fruit, but their roots run deep.

The roots are in my soul. What does a fucking computer know about that?"

"Do I look like a hairdresser to you? I'm a real man. This arm. Do you see this arm?" the pirate says, pointing to where a real arm used to be. "What do you think caused that? The Indians got ahold of me. They cut off my arm."

"You think that's manly. Huh? You think that's manly. One day I outwitted thirteen bloodhounds."

"Preposterous."

"I did. Thirteen bloodhounds. They had me up a tree."

"That can't be. I've studied the history of bloodhounds since the age of William the Conqueror, and that's just a niggardly lie."

"What did you say?"

"I said it's just a niggardly lie."

"Why, you—" Quickskill rushes around the desk and nabs the pirate, lifting him up.

They begin to struggle. The pirate delivers a stunning blow to Quickskill's jaw. Quickskill comes back with a thunderous right uppercut, sending the pirate reeling against the boat's rails. Quaw Quaw begins to scream. The pirate comes off the rail with a crushing blow to the forehead of Quickskill. Stunned, Quickskill shakes his head, and before the pirate is about to follow through, knocks the wind out of him with a short, savage right to the stomach, and then . . . a splash! They stop. Quaw Quaw is nowhere in sight.

They run to the direction of the splash and look over the rail. Quaw Quaw is swimming, moving away from the ship, in the treacherous rapids of the Niagara River.

Her clothes were in a small pile next to their feet. They yelled after her until their voices became hoarse. They yelled that mournful, pining Chloe yell. Chloe. Originally the haunting moan of the slave seeking his lost wife—Chloe.

24

The pirate was serving Quickskill out of a silver champagne goblet. Quickskill was sitting at the table, staring straight ahead.

"Now we've both lost her," said the pirate matter-of-factly.

"You haven't lost anything. What was she to you, Jack? Something you could sequin and polish. A subhuman pagan you sent to Radcliffe to learn to appreciate twelve-tone music when her people's scales were more complex, to appreciate nature poetry when her people were one with the bear and the fish and the mountains and the waters, to appreciate uptown classical painting when one totem out front was as good as anything inside." Quickskill watched Jack take a sip. "You can always write her off as a loss, like all the other items you ship out that get damaged or fall from trucks onto the freeway."

"No, you're wrong, Quickskill. I have emotions too. That's what's wrong with your argument. You think you're the only one with heart, with soul. I have feelings. I am not desensitized. I love her, in my own way. That night when I first saw her and captured her during the raid on her father's village, she was a beautiful treasure to me. And there was great opposition to our marriage. From both sides. I had to send out thirty stereos and fifty mink coats to cool out the gossip. And I didn't object to her affairs. I knew that her blood wasn't like mine: cold, Anglo-Saxon. She had a different temperature and often, well, I was too busy. But you . . . Whatever you had going between you, it was too deep."

"Well, it's late. Maybe I'll climb into a canoe and go back to Buffalo. Stay in the Eagle Tavern for the night. Head out to Canada tomorrow."

"You can't return."

"Why?"

"Swille's men are all over town. They're in cahoots with the Buffalo Anti-Subversive Squad. A.S.S. Those fat men you see hobbling up and down the aisles taking notes and talking into walkie-talkies at anti-slavery meetings. They'll certainly lock you up in the Erie County jail for the night. Then take you back to 'Ginny. You don't want to go back to 'Ginny, do you? I understand that the worst torture a black can get is 'Virginia Play.' Isn't that what they call it? 'Virginia Play.' I'll take you across. This yacht has a thirty-thousand-dollar motor."

"You know, Jack, you're not such a bad guy. What's wrong with you? Why are you . . . I mean, so mean. Raiding villages. Plundering . . ."

"I was young then."

"But even now. Why do you tie up things so? Not permitting a free flow of ideas."

"Somebody's got to do it. Emerson, Thoreau, Greeley. Soft white men. Swille had his points. I used to admire him. But now he's behind. Still thinking that he can maintain his empire through flogging and killing. It's made him depraved."

"You're telling me. He has this private projection room where he shows films of slaves being tortured, pilloried, castrated, and he and his guests sit around sipping black milkshakes; it . . ."

"You see." He goes over, picks up the phone and orders one of his men to begin the journey toward Niagara Falls, Ontario.

"Would you like something to eat, Quickskill? Lasagne?

Crêpe cannelloni? Besciamella? I have some fine pastas I can order up."

"No, thanks."

They finally reached the other side. A man was waiting to canoe Quickskill to the banks. Yankee Jack had phoned ahead. Raven put his gear over his shoulder. He picked up his suitcase.

"Well, this is it." The pirate extended his hand.

Quickskill looked at it. "I don't think so. Thanks for the ride, but if I ever meet you on free ground, I'm going to kill you."

The pirate chuckled. "Have it your way."

Quickskill climbs into the canoe. The man prepares to row to the shore.

"One more thing," the pirate says. "I read your poem 'Third World Belle.' It was a giveaway. One thing, though. You said I buried her brother in a sealed-off section of the Metropolitan Museum. Wrong. It was the Museum of Natural History. One of the board members, an old friend, Captain Kidd, had called me in to be a co-consultant on an Oceanic exhibit they were giving. Well, her brother rushed past the guard and into the board room to complain about a statue they have outside of Theodore Roosevelt sitting on a horse while a black slave and an Indian are obsequiously kneeling next to it, like the President's children. He said it was paternalistic. He said something about its being racist. He had a shotgun, and . . . well, we couldn't have him waving that thing around. We had to, ah, subdue him, and I guess we used a little too much force. We didn't want to carry out the body before all of those milling visitors and so we stuffed him and put him downstairs in the lower floor. He's there now, standing in a huge log boat next to a shaman figure."

Quickskill wasn't listening. The boat began to move toward land. Soon Quickskill would be free. But he was too tired and depressed to greet this prospect with joyful exclamation of former slaves who reached this moment of Jubilation.

"While they were on my vessel I felt little interest in them, and had no idea that the love of liberty as a part of man's nature was in the least possible degree felt or understood by them. Before entering Buffalo harbor, I ran in near the Canada shore, manned a boat and landed them on the beach . . . They said, 'Is this Canada?' I said, 'Yes, there are no slaves in this country'; then I witnessed a scene I shall never forget. They seemed to be transformed; a new light shone in their eyes, their tongues were loosed, they laughed and cried, prayed and sang praises, fell upon the ground and kissed it, hugged and kissed each other, crying, 'Bress de Lord! Oh! I'se free before I die!' "

25

Raven Quickskill was sitting on the terrace of the Queen Victoria Gardens Hotel in Niagara Falls, Ontario, Canada. He had to wait for a while to get a seat. He was looking out on the indescribable American Falls. It was the closest spot to heaven on earth. People of all races, classes, descriptions seemed to be there, dangling their feet on the walls overlooking the slopes, which ran down to the two-lane highway and to the rails where people of all ages looked out at the wonder, the terrifying rapids below. Was all of Canada like this? Then he saw it. The crowd looked up.

He could make out some kind of figure in the mist. It was a figure on a tightrope. The figure seemed to be carrying a banner. Later he was to learn that the tightrope was eleven hundred feet long, one hundred and sixty feet above the water. People closed in about the railing for a closer look. The patrons of the hotel rose from their seats and went down the slope to look, too. He joined them. He was curious. People were shoving each other to get to one of the telescopes that one could employ, near the rails.

He found an empty one and looked through. It was a woman. She was in Indian clothes. She was coming across Niagara Falls. She was walking on a tightrope across Niagara Falls!

Sam Patch must be rolling in the grave, he thought. A woman doing this. She was doing what no man had ever done. She was coming across, backward. Quaw Quaw! He could tell it was she because he knew her backward quite well. It could be nobody else's backward but hers. Carrying the banner, she did a somersault. The crowd gaped and murmured. It said *Ahhhhhh*. Later she said she would have made two omelettes, breaking the eggs in midair, but she figured that would be too anti-suffragette. All the way up in the air, doing housework. She kept coming across the tightrope as the crowd on both sides grew hushed. It even seemed that the Falls had hushed. It was an "eerie quiet." Would she make it?

Of course, now he understood what she meant. Blondinist. He had thought it was some new rebellion game invented by the *Emancipation Bugle*.

Blondin. French tightrope walker. "The Little Wonder." Jean François Gravelet. Walked above the Falls on a tightrope in 1859. She had done him better. Her feat was like her life, between the American and Canadian Falls with a gorge underneath. They argued all the time, but this they had in common. He was the raven. *Ga! Ga! Gaaa! Ga!* They both were capable of producing cliff-hangers, as she was now.

She reached the other side and the crowd went wild, joining hands and jumping about, whistling, stomping their feet. Automobiles were honking, policemen were blowing whistles. She had reached the other side and was coming down.

He could then read the banner she carried: *Quickskill, I love you.*

26

Later they were dining in the Victoria Gardens restaurant. She had gone upstairs to her suite to change, a difficult feat because the lobby was crowded with the press and with people from television and radio. The Canadian police had to help her to her room. He waited for her downstairs in the restaurant. Finally, when she appeared again, she was wearing a grey somber-striped Happi coat made of sheared weasel, which she had bought on impulse from the money collected when the hat was passed among the spectators. People had made movie offers. Book contracts were proposed. She turned them all down, telling the people that she was an "artist" and that she was "pure" and that she "didn't want to sell out."

Now it was quieter. People only glanced their way from time to time. They were alone. She was telling him her adventures, which occurred after she dove into the Niagara.

"Well, I swam and swam, and it was getting very dark and there was a fisherman. He noticed me and he asked if I wanted to be pulled out of the water. He said if I continued, I'd be swept over the falls. Well, my mind wasn't into that, I was just swimming. I didn't have any destination in mind; I heard the roar in the distance, but I didn't know it was Niagara Falls. Then it occurred to me, I had a chance to do Blondin one better. I would walk the tightrope across Niagara Falls backwards. Well, the fisherman provided me with some blankets. He was very nice about it. He got me to the shore and hailed a cab for me. I came to this hotel and got a suite."

"How did you do that? You didn't have any money."

"Oh, Mother just bought a forest up here. I simply told them who I was. No trouble. They called Mother and she told them to give me what I wanted. They're used to Americans owning forests, lakes and mountains up here."

"You've always gotten what you wanted, haven't you?"

"Just about. Anyway, I bought some clothes and supplies and then a couple of long rolls of wire. I had some workmen hitch it up to some poles, and just as the tourists began arriving this morning I started out."

"You're crazy," he said playfully, smiling.

"No, not crazy, famous. If I'd slipped and fallen, then I would have been crazy."

"Hey, look," Quickskill said, "it's Carpenter."

And it was Carpenter. He was in the lobby, registering in the hotel. His head was bandaged, and he walked with the assistance of a cane. Quickskill rose and went to the lobby. He brought Carpenter back to the table.

"Carpenter, how are you? What happened?" Quaw Quaw said, rising.

Carpenter pulled up a chair. Ordered some Scotch.

"Cutty Sark?" the waitress asked.

"No, not me," he said, waving her away, "Ballantine. I don't want anything to do with Canada. The sooner I'm out of here the better."

"What on earth happened, man?" Quickskill asked.

"Some mobocrats beat me up," he said, pointing to the bandages on his head. "Left me in the street unconscious. I was going back to the hotel after being denied this room I wanted to rent."

"In Canada? You were denied a room?" Quickskill asked.

"That's right. Man, I'd take my chance with Nebraskaites, Know-Nothings and Democrats anytime. Even a Copperhead or a Confederate."

"I don't understand, Carpenter. Why, outside it looks like the Peaceable Kingdom."

"Maybe here but not elsewhere. Man, as soon as you reach the metropolitan areas you run into Ford, Sears, Holiday Inn, and all the rest."

"You're kiddin," Quickskill said. "You have to be kiddin."

"Cross my heart and hope to die."

"But what about St. Catherine's? William Wells Brown told me that he'd gotten a number of slaves across to St. Catherine's, where they found rewarding careers."

"Let me show you downtown St. Catherine's," Carpenter said, removing a photo from his wallet. It looked like any American strip near any American airport; it could have been downtown San Mateo. Neon signs with clashing letters advertising hamburgers, used-car lots with the customary banners, coffee joints where you had to stand up and take your java from wax cups.

"It looks so aesthetically unsatisfying."

"You can say that again, Quaw Quaw," Quickskill said.

"Man, they got a group up here called the Western Guard, make the Klan look like statesmen. Vigilantes harass fugitive slaves, and the slaves have to send their children to schools where their presence is subject to catcalls and harassment. Don't go any farther, especially with her. They beat up Chinamen and Pakastani in the streets. West Indians they shoot."

"I'm a Native American," she said.

Quickskill had never heard her say it that way. A Native American. And she stuck out her chest.

"Don't you remember her, Carpenter? She came to your party."

"Oh, that's right. I was a little high that night. Don't remember everybody who came. Was so glad to get to Canada. Now look. Man, let me show you something." Carpenter pulled from his pocket a piece of paper upon which some figures had been written. "Of the ten top Canadian corporations, four are dominated by American interests. Americans control fifty-five percent of sales of manufactured goods and make sixty-three percent of the profits. They receive fifty-five percent of mining sales and forty percent of paper sales. Man, Americans own Canada. They just permit Canadians to operate it for them. They needs a Castro up here bad. And get this. *Time* magazine receives special tax rates up here."

The more Carpenter continued to talk, the more depressed Quickskill became.

Finally Carpenter got up from his seat. "Well, Quickskill, Quaw Quaw, I have to go," he said, downing his Scotch. "Want to get up early in the morning to start the journey back to Emancipation. Those people I sublet my apartment to are really going to be in for a surprise."

"Yeah, sure, Carpenter," Quickskill said in almost a whisper.

"See you back in Emancipation . . . Oh yeah, I forgot to tell you . . ."

"What's that?"

"Swille got his."

"What do you mean?"

"It was in the newspapers. His old lady burned him."

"That's nice."

"What? I expected to hear a bigger response than that."

"To tell you the truth, I don't really care at this point, Carpenter. After what you've said about Canada. All my life I had hopes about it, that whatever went wrong I would always have Canada to go to."

"Don't let it get you down, Raven. Look, I'd better be going."

Carpenter left a tip, and using his cane, headed toward the elevator.

"Quickskill," Quaw Quaw said, reaching out her hand to him, "don't take it so hard. Quickskill . . ."

But Quickskill held his head between his hands. Then he slowly dropped his head to the table and let it rest there for a while, his arms stretched out.

27

He felt his guts were made of aluminum. The tears went to behind his eyes and burned there. She had her black silky Indian hair resting on his shoulder. Her arm was inside his. From time to time she'd pinch his arm. He'd look at her and smile. There were fruit stands on the highway. Red apples, yellow grapefruit. Fresh. She'd want to stop and buy some. Good-eyes Raven would point to a cloud in the direction opposite that of the fruit stand. He didn't feel like stopping.

"Look, there's a cloud," he'd say.

"Where? I don't see it."

It worked every time. They were approaching the border. There was a long line of cars. The border was tense, and some of the passengers stood beside the vehicles. They were being questioned by the border guards. The United States still hadn't gotten over that incident which took place during the War of 1812. The Canadians had tried to burn down the White House. The Canadians hadn't forgotten that they had repelled three invasions from the Union. A fortnight before, the Prime Minister of Canada had publicly rebuked an American ambassador for having "overstepped the bounds of diplomatic propriety."

Things brimmed over when a visiting American producer

and director had called the National Arts Center's theatre in Ottawa "lousy," and suggested that whoever built it "should be shot." The next day the Château Laurier in Ottawa was blown up. Some blamed it on "Seceshes," an abundance of which every nation has. Others said it sounded like Yankees. The "staid" London *Times* had described the Yankee character as one of "swagger" and "ferocity," this after Captain Charles Wilkes of the Union ship *San Jacinto* had boarded England's *Trent* in order to arrest two Confederate diplomats. It was described as an "audacious" act which outraged the "civilized world."

Had crossing the Atlantic changed the character of both Europeans and Africans? Were Yankees really "vulgar cowards" as the London *Times* had said? Why had the Canadian Prime Minister said that living next to the Union was like being a flea on an elephant? Every time the elephant twitched you felt it. Why did the Europeans think that Yankees hunted elephants?

They weren't surprised, therefore, when a kid-glove-wearing guard in a black bear coat waved them over to the side. He walked to their car and peeked in. Noticing Quaw Quaw, he asked, "Hey, aren't you one of them Japs who used to worship dragons and were in the throes of superstition?" It wasn't said with any malice. He was friendly even, and when he said it, smiled at both of them. He then removed a handbook from his pocket. "Japs, Japs. J . . . Japs," he said, leafing through. "The Union is a Christian Union, and there's no room for infidels."

"She's not Japanese, she's Indian."

But by this time Quaw Quaw had leaped out of the car and was heading toward the guard, her face contorted in anger, like a mask he had once seen.

The guard dropped his pencil and stepped back. "Wait a minute. Aren't you the girl who walked across Niagara Falls on a tightrope? Quaw Quaw Tralaralara."

When they heard that, the passengers of the other cars stopped honking and rushed out of their cars with matchbox covers, napkins, candy-bar wrappers, pads, driver's licenses and anything they could find to get Quaw Quaw's autograph. For someone who talked about how she "disdained" commercialism and how her Columbia professors had taught her to "deplore" the "star system," she seemed to be enjoying it. Well, at least to Quickskill she seemed to be enjoying it. Only one of Quaw Quaw's fans recognized him, and then only to ask him for a piece of paper to write Quaw Quaw's name on.

Later they were driving toward the Eagle Hotel when Quaw Quaw said, "Weren't they wonderful? Did you see how they swarmed about me? They love me, Raven! They love me!" She stretched her arms. "I'm out in the open now. Only me and an audience. Put in the open where dance should be. Where it's always been."

"Yeah, out in the open, all right. You seemed to lick it up. All of that open. Them loving you. I thought you were so abstract. A 'pure' artist you always said. Not a 'star.' That's what you always said. Anyway, don't you think walking on a tightrope across the Falls was a cheap stunt? Now all of the dancers in New York will be coming up here walking across the damned Falls. Making this . . . this supreme wonder into a sideshow. Long articles in the magazine sections of small-town newspapers. You belong to that pirate. You're just like him. Only he's honest with his. You're an ambitious mountain climber. Only this time it's the mountain of success."

"How corny, 'the mountain of success.' And you're a poet you think. And you use lines like 'the mountain of success.' You ought to study the 'masters' and then you won't be so given to using lines like the mountain of success. You . . . you . . ."

"Go on and say it. Barbarian. That's what you want to say, isn't it? Pocahontas, that's what you are. Turn in your own father for a pirate . . ."

"That's not the way the story goes. Not only are you stupid, Raven, you're inaccurate. Raven. Your name ought to be turkey. That's what you are, a turkey. Drowned because he's too stupid to bend his head from the raining sky. You turkey."

"Don't call me a turkey."

"You fucking shithead turkey, turkey! Turkey! Turkey!" She started screaming. He removed one hand from the steering wheel and was about to slap her when he saw their commotion had gotten some traveling spectators. She and her Blondin thing were going too far.

"Look, when we go back to the Eagle, why don't you return to your neo-Feudalistic life with your husband and sit around with his decadent pro-Gothic friends dining on caviar and discussing Chopin, Soho and birds like that, and eating mandarin fish and light-jeweled pigeon." She had folded her arms and was sulking. "And another thing. Whenever someone confuses you with some other race, why don't you tell them you don't care about race and that you don't have time to fool around with such subjects as race; and that you don't identify with any group. Ha. Tell them you don't identify with any group."

He looked at her. She was staring straight ahead. She stared vacantly like that until they reached the Eagle Hotel.

When he checked in there was a note for him from Uncle Robin. The next morning he received another note. Her note. In the middle of the night, while he was sleeping, she had left the hotel.

28

". . . and to Moe, my white house slave, I leave my checker-board and my checkers because, you see, we found it was a sport he enjoys. We found out that it was Moe who was taking my wine and distributing it at these singles parties he had for the white slaves. I knew about these parties because I had Nebraska Tracers to bug the motel rooms and install two-way mirrors where these free-wheeling affairs were held. He's an expense-account rogue, too."

Moe's collar must have become tight because he started fidgeting with it. Some soft chuckling could be heard from those who had gathered for the reading of Swille's will—the household staff and his relatives, two brothers and a sister, Anne, who were dressed, dignified, in millionaire-black. Uncle Robin sat next to Aunt Judy. He was gazing at the ceiling. His arms were folded. He was whistling very softly to himself.

"Otherwise, Moe has served me long and hard, and so in order to soften this insult I leave him Blue Cross, Blue Shield, old-age pension, paid vacations, Christmas and New Year's off, an annual ticket to the circus, coffee breaks, a scholarship for two of his children, a year's supply of Scotch tape, two hunting dogs, and a partridge in a pear tree . . .

Then the Judge paused. What could be wrong? He must

have stared at the document for a full minute. He peered at
it over his glasses. He removed his glasses and blinked his eyes.
He put them on again. He scratched his head. His mouth
opened wide. He began to stutter and rattle the paper in his
trembling hands.

"And to Uncle Robin, I leave this Castle, these hills and
everything behind the gates of the Swille Virginia estate."

Much commotion. The Judge called for silence. Moe
slumped in his chair, the checkers dropping from their box,
falling red and black to the floor. He stooped to gather them.
Mammy Barracuda stood and shook her fist in Robin's direction. Cato the Graffado pleaded with her to sit down. "We
might not get nothing, Mammy." She sat down.

The Judge turned to Robin. "Robin, I've known you a
long time. You've gotten the trust of the Planters. We all
admire you about these parts."

"I deem it a pleasure to be so fortunate that God would
ordain that I, a humble African, would be so privileged as to
have a home in Virginia like this one. Why, your Honor, it's
like paradise down here. The sun just kinda lazily dropping in
the evening sky. The lugubrious, voluptuous tropical after-
noons make me swoon, Judge. Make me swoon."

"Very poetical, Robin. Very poetical," the Judge said.
"Then you won't take offense if I ask you a delicate question?"

"What's that, Judge?"

"Science says . . . well, according to science, Robin, the
Negro doesn't . . . well, your brain—it's about the size of a
mouse's. This is a vast undertaking. Are you sure you can
handle it? Juggling figures. Filling out forms."

"I've watched Massa Swille all these many years, your
Honor. Watching such a great genius—a one-in-a-million genius like Massa Swille—is like going to Harvard and Yale at the
same time and Princeton on weekends. My brains has grown,
Judge. My brains has grown watching Massa Swille all these
years."

Then turning to Swille's relatives, Robin stood, tearfully.
"I'm going to run it just like my Massa run it," he said, clasping

his hands and gazing toward the ceiling. "If the Good Lord would let me live without my Massa— Oh, what I going to do without him? But if the Lord 'low me to continue—"

Cato muttered, "Allow, allow," putting his hand to his forehead and slowly bringing it down over his face in embarrassment.

"If I can just go on, I'm going to try to make Massa Swille up in hebbin proud of me."

Ms. Anne Swille rose. "Oh, Judge, don't be mean to Robin. Let him have it. My brother would have wanted it this way. It's in the will."

Donald Swille, the banker, rose too. "Yes, Judge. Uncle Robin is quite capable of managing this land. My brother always spoke highly of his abilities. I'm sure he can manage it. My brother often said he didn't know what he'd do without Robin. That Robin treated him as though he were a god. This is the least the Family can do for Robin's long service," Donald Swille said, resting his hand on Robin's shoulder. Robin, his head in his hands, was being comforted by Aunt Judy.

"So be it," the Judge said.

He continued the reading of the will. Aunt Judy cuddled up next to Robin, who stared straight ahead, his eyes dry, unfazed by the whispers going on about him.

"I have set aside a quantity of land in Washington, D.C., for the erection of a Christian training school for the newly liberated slaves, who, without some moral code, will revert to their African ways and customs known to be barbarous and offensive to the civilized sensibility. In this school, Mammy Barracuda will see to it that the students are austere and abstemious. So that this school might be truly structured, I leave my closetful of precious whips and all of my fettering devices to Mammy."

With that, Mammy Barracuda lit up, raising her feet from the floor. She rubbed her hands and smiled at Cato.

"And my final request may sound a little odd to the Yankees who've invaded our bucolic haven, but I wish to be buried in my sister's sepulcher by the sea, joined in the Kama

Sutra position below . . ."—the Judge blushed as he examined the illustration on the document—"that we may be joined together in eternal and sweet Death."

The reading was over. Mammy Barracuda and the rest of the house people, including Moe, walked out. Others came up to congratulate Robin. Pompey was last.

"Hey, Uncle Robin, that's nice," he said, grinning.

Swille's brothers came to congratulate Robin on his good fortune and to comment upon their brother's philanthropy. The sister, Anne, shook his hand and smiled behind her veil. They headed out of the Castle toward their limousines.

29

The next morning Uncle Robin and Aunt Judy were having their first breakfast in their new home. The whippoorwills were chirping outside. In the distance a Negro harmonica could be heard twanging dreamily.

"Isn't it amazing," Aunt Judy said, lifting a mouthful of pancake with her silver fork, "last night we were in the Frederick Douglass Houses and now we're in the Master's Castle."

"An incredible reversal of fortune, but not as incredible as it may seem. You know the expression Mammy Barracuda used to say, 'God helps those who helps themselves.' Well, sometimes the god that's fast for them is slow or even indifferent to us, so we have to call on our own gods who work for us as fast as theirs works for them. When we came here, our gods came with us. They'll never go away. No slavemaster can make them go away. They won't budge from this soil."

"I don't follow, Robin."

"I dabbled with the will. I prayed to one of our gods, and he came to me in a dream. He was wearing a top hat, raggedy britches and an old black opera waistcoat. He had on alligator shoes. He was wearing that top hat, too, and was puffing on a cigar. Look like Lincoln's hat. That stovepipe. He said it was okay to do it. The 'others' had approved." Uncle Robin poured some syrup on a pancake. "He asked me for a drink and a cigar."

"Okay to do what, Robin?"

"To dabble with the will. He said that we should work Taneyism right back on him."

"I don't understand, Robin," Judy said, pouring a cup of coffee from one of Swille's pitchers.

"Taney was that old man with twisted locks who used to dress up like the Masque of the Red Death and was born with a twisted lip under his left eye. The one who said that Dred Scott was property. Well, if they are not bound to respect our rights, then I'll be damned if we should respect theirs. Fred Douglass said the same thing. Well, anyway, Swille had something called dyslexia. Words came to him scrambled and jumbled. I became his reading and writing. Like a computer, only this computer left itself Swille's whole estate. Property joining forces with property. I left me his whole estate. I'm it, too. Me and it got more it."

"But, Robin, isn't that somewhat un-Christian?"

"I've about had it with this Christian. I mean, it can stay, but it's going to have to stop being so bossy. I'd like to bring the old cults back. This Christian isn't going to work for us. It's for desert people. Grey, arid, cold. It's a New Mexico religion. There's not a cloud there often, and when they do come, it looks like judgment. Sure was lively out in the woods when they had them horn cults, blacks dressed up like Indians. Everybody could act a fool, under controlled conditions."

"I don't follow you sometimes, Robin, but what you say makes a lot of sense."

"It's all in those books and newspapers. You want to learn?"

"To read and write?"

"Yes."

"You'd teach me?"

"Sure. We can start next week."

"That's wonderful, Robin."

She rose and began to clear the table. Bangalang came in.

"You sit down, girl," she said to Judy. "That's my job. You're not the head of the kitchen any more. You're supposed to raise lilacs, sew flags and have teas for the ladies nearby."

Judy looked angry. "I don't need you to take care of my table. I'll take care of it. I'm not Ms. Swille. I'd go out of my mind if I had to go through what she did."

"Let Bangalang do it for now, Judy. I'll think of something," Robin said.

"Well, you'd better. You're not going to make me no belle. I wasn't cut out to be no belle. Fluttering my eyelashes. Japanese fans."

"Speaking of belles, Judy, Ms. Swille will be out of the sanitarium next week. The Judge told me when he gave me the first monthly stock check."

"That's nice. Is she going to stay here?" Judy asked, sipping from the one cup of coffee Bangalang left behind.

"No, she's gotten a job in a Toronto museum as part of a super-rich rehabilitation program. Guess what her first project is, Judy."

"What, Robin?"

"Creating a replica of a Virginia plantation. Strange world, isn't it, Judy?"

"Strange indeed," Judy said, lighting a cigarette. "I wonder did she really push him into the fire?"

"We'll never know. Those distinguished parapsychologists got her off. That evidence they provided was impressive. What they said about Ectoplasm and Etheric Doubles. Etheric Doubles. I sure hope I don't run into my Etheric Double if it's in the same condition as Ms. Vivian. That Etheric Double was out for blood if Ms. Swille is telling the truth."

"If anything could come up out of the grave, it would be that Vivian. Bangalang said that Swille's daddy, Swille II, was poisoned by that old hateful green-eyed girl. That he just didn't die of natural causes. Bangalang hinted that Swille II and that old evil gal were engaged in . . . in . . . Lot's sin. Bangalang told only me. She was scared that she knew."

"Oh, that's just Bangalang. You know how she talks. But

then again, it's really immoral down here. Andrew Johnson
called it that. An immoral land. The devil's country home.
That's what the South is. It's where the devil goes to rest after
he's been about the world wearying the hunted and the
haunted. This is the land of the hunted and haunted. This is
where he comes. The devil sits on the porch of his plantation.
He's dressed up like a gentleman and sitting on a white porch
between some white columns. All the tormented are out in
fields, picking cotton and tobacco and looking after his swine,
who have human heads and scales on their pig legs and make
pitiful cries as they are whipped. And the devil just grins,
sitting there on his devil's porch. Rocking. Rocking like the
devil rocks. And that old wicked Quantrell, his overseer, with
his blazing Simon Legree blue eyes, is whipping a malnutri-
tioned woman for the devil's entertainment. And the devil
laughs his ungodly laugh. And the woman is Lawrence Kansas.
And there's blood coming from Lawrence Kansas' mouth. This
is the devil's vacation spot where he personally takes care of all
the reservations and arranges for the tour buses to reach various
parts of Virginia Hell. Immoral is too polite a word. Devildom.
Virginia is where the devil reigns. Can we save Virginia?"

Pompey stands at the doorway; he holds a pillow bearing
a silver telephone. "Uncle Robin, telephone. Says it's Harriet
Beecher Stowe calling from Jewett Publishers in Boston."

"Uncle Robin?"

"Yes."

*"This is Harriet Beecher Stowe, calling from the plush-
carpeted walnut-wooded offices of Jewett Publishers in Boston."*

"Yes, my employee told me."

*"Your . . . er . . . man? Yes, of course, I did read where
Arthur Swille left you his entire fortune. What was wrong with
him?"*

"I don't understand, Ms. Stowe. Mr. Swille was a good
man. We were all fond of him down here."

*"Oh yes, of course. Look, I'm putting together an anthol-
ogy of slave poetry. Can you tell me where I can find Henry
Bibb?"*

"I'm not exactly the ledger keeper for all of the fugitives in the world, but I think you might find him in Canada these days, Ms. Stowe."

"Well, I hope he's playing the harp for Christ and not up to his bad habits. Is he still refusing to talk to white people?"

". . . . ."

"Uncle Robin . . . by the way, are you the Uncle Robin I interviewed for my book?"

"Yes, Ms. Stowe. You gave me a pig, a duck and a goose. Remember?"

"Yes, well, Uncle Robin, I'd like to do a book on you . . . and what it felt like being the house man of one of the most rich and fabulous men in the world. Known everywhere as the American Baron."

"I got somebody already, Ms. Stowe."

"You have somebody? Who could you know?"

"Raven Quickskill. He's going to do it."

"But I've already told Mr. Jewett that you'd do it for me. I need to buy a new silk dress. I have to go to England . . . I . . ."

Robin hangs up.

"What was that all about?" Aunt Judy said.

"Nothing, dear," Robin said.

"Robin?"

"Yes, dear?"

"There was something I always meant to ask you. But I figured it was your business. It always struck me as being curious."

"What, dear?"

"Why did you provide that man with those poor slave mothers' milk each morning? That was hard to swallow. But you were my husband and so I never brought it up," Aunt Judy said, squashing her Turkish cigarette in one of Swille's ashtrays.

"That wasn't slave mothers' milk," Uncle Robin said, puffing on a Brazilian cigar. "That was Coffee Mate,"* he said,

---

*Corn-syrup solids, vegetable fat, sodium caseinate, mono- and diglycerides, dipotassium phosphate, sodium silicoaluminate, artificial flavor, tricalcium phosphate, and artificial colors.

blowing out smoke rings. "Every time I went on trips for Swille, I'd load up on it. They serve it on the airplanes. I'm an old hand at poisons, and so I'd venture a guess that if Swille's wife, or Vivian or whatever or whoever pushed him hadn't he'd of 'gone on' from the cumulative effects of the Coffee Mate. Cartwright ain't the only scientist. Those Double Etherics that Ms. Swille's defense witnesses talked about sounded more scientific than that bull he been laying down. I was keeping busy around here, and now that Swille's finished I think I'll return to my old job, and let Pompey handle the figures. It's about time he learned. The boy's fast. He's so fast that some of the people are talking about seeing him in two places at the same time. He's a good voice-thrower too. He's got a little act he entertains us with. He puts on animal clothes and will do an impersonation of any animal you know. If you want him to be an eagle, he'll get up and flap his wings and jump up and down. If you want him to be a turtle, he'll walk ponderously about on all fours and do his neck like a rubbery telescope. The other night he dressed up like a low-budget peacock. He can do impersonations too. He got the whole Swille family down pat. He can do all of the men and women, and the dead ones too. His room is full of all kinds of animal and reptile and bird masks. I'm going to let him juggle the books around here for a while. Then I can go back to my plants. The camellias, the azaleas, and the ones only I know."

"Robin," Aunt Judy said, rising slowly from the table, "I think I'll go upstairs. What are we going to do with all of this space, Robin? We're not used to living like this. All we need is an apartment. They say there are fifty rooms in this place. What are we going to do with fifty rooms? Fifty rooms will be hard to clean, Robin."

"You have servants. Bangalang."

"I don't want Bangalang in my house. Robin, you're going to have to do something. You got us into this."

"I told you I'll think of something, Judy. You go on upstairs. I have a lot of thinking to do."

She walks over to where he's sitting and kisses him on the cheek. "I know you'll think of something."

She walks out of the room and up the stairs. Robin rises, goes over to the liquor cabinet, pours himself a double bourbon, walks over to the window. A car is moving up the driveway. Who could this be?

There's a knock at the door. Robin opens it. It's Stray Leechfield and two men, one short and one medium.

"Would you get your man Master Arthur Swille; we'll wait here in the lobby," the short one said, removing his hat, walking a grumbling Stray Leechfield into the hall. The medium one was handcuffed to Leechfield.

"I'm afraid my man is dead," Robin said, bowing his head. "I'm the man here now."

"He died? What does that mean?" the medium one said, staring at his companion.

"It means that I'm free. Now will you take these handcuffs off?" Leechfield said, stretching out his hands. "I have to get to New York for the opening of the Leechfield & Leer Minstrel Organization at the Ethiopian Opera House on Broadway," Leechfield said, his nose to the ceiling.

"What's so funny?" Leechfield said, glaring at Uncle Robin. Leechfield was dressed in a white Russian drill coat, ruby-red plush breeches, a beautiful cloth waistcoat of the color of ideal sky-blue, a splendid silk shirt and a rakish French hat from New Orleans. He had rings on all of his fingers, a diamond stickpin on a cravat and Wellington boots.

"Man, is that the way you dress up around the Great Lakes?" Robin asked.

"It's my bi'ness how I dress, old man," Leechfield said. "You ain't bound to me. You don't have to identify with me. Why don't you get free, old man? Then maybe you'll let me be free. You ought to get out of the South once in a while. Then you'd know that these are theatrical clothes. Dummy. This what theatrical people wear out there in the smart world."

"Let him go," Robin said. "It's all right."

"Yeah, but with Swille gone, who's going to pay the bill?"

"Yeah, who's going to pay the bill?" the medium one said.

"I'll pay. I've taken over the books. I'll give you a check,"

Robin said. "But first, I know you've traveled far for this. Why don't you go into the kitchen and have Bangalang fix you some sandwiches and give you a bottle of beer."

The three start for the kitchen, led by Leechfield. Being a former Greaser, he knows where the kitchen is.

"Hold on, Leechfield," Robin says.

"Yeah, what is it?" Leechfield says with a sneer.

"Did you really think that it was just a matter of economics? Did you think you could just hand history a simple check, that you could short-change history, and history would let you off as simple as that? You've insulted history, Leechfield. The highest insult! You thought he'd let you off with a simple check. It was more complicated than that. You thought you were dealing with straw when you're dealing with iron. He was going to return you the check. He had money. He didn't want money. He wanted the slave in you. When you defied him, took off, the money was no longer the issue. He couldn't conceive of a world without slaves. That was his grand scheme. A world of lords, ladies and slaves. You were showing the other slaves that it didn't have to be that way. That the promised land was in their heads. The old way. The old way taught that man could be the host for God. Not one man. All men. That was the conflict between you and Swille. You, 40s and Quickskill threatened to give the god in the slave breath."

"I don't know what you and Quickskill are talking about. House talk. Talk from the living room of ideas. He didn't take the check. It doesn't matter now. He's dead. I wasn't doing all that when I ran away. Not what you said. I not only ran away from the Master, but from the slaves too. Sometimes it was hard for me to tell the difference. I got whips from both of them. I decided to do it for a living. As you can see from my clothes and from my newly acquired wealth, it's a thriving industry. Anyway, you keep doing it, Uncle Robin." Leechfield left for the kitchen.

Robin smiled. That Leechfield is a flambeau carrier in a Mardi Gras parade.

*   *   *

The violet sun was setting behind the Virginia hills. Soon it would be night. A night so black the stars looked like scattered sugar crystals.

That was a strange letter from Raven this morning. I'm glad he's doing my book. I'll be glad to see him again. I wonder did he find what he was looking for in Canada? Probably all that freedom gets to you. Too much freedom makes you lazy. Nothing to fight. Well, I guess Canada, like freedom, is a state of mind. Them counts and earls look like they're free, but they're not free. Always in the newspapers caught with their baby dolls. Old Abe showed them, though. What a player. Abe showed those dukes and earls. Old Jeff Davis in jail, doomed to be the name on a dirt road in crawfish country, Louisiana.

What happened to all they Canadas? Quickskill, 40s, Leechfield, Davis, Swille, old Abe. Old Abe gunned down while watching a comedy. Gunned down by one of those true savages, dressed in zealot's popinjay clothes. Maybe Raven can talk about all of that. Glad my letter reached him up at the Eagle Hotel. Old Pompey knew. How did Pompey know? What a strange one. Knew where Raven was. Like he flew my letter to Raven at the Eagle Hotel. What did Raven mean when he said, "Writing always catches up with me"? Quickskill—that boy has tried to be so clear. He'll always be a poet, that Raven.

I couldn't do for no Canada. Not me. I'm too old. I done had my Canadas. I'm like the fellow who, when they asked why he sent for a helicopter to get him out of prison, answered, "I was too old to go over the wall." That's the way I feel. Too old to go over the wall. Somebody had to stay. Might as well have been me and Judy. Yeah, they get down on me an Tom. But who's the fool? Nat Turner or us? Nat said he was going to do this. Was going to do that. Said he had a mission. Said his destiny was a divine one. Said that fate had chosen him. That the gods were handling him and speaking through him. Now Nat's dead and gone for these many years, and here I am master of a dead man's house. Which one is the fool? One who has been dead for these many years or a master in a dead man's house. I'll bet they'll be trying to figure that one out for a long time. A long, long time.

Well, you had to hand it to Swille. He was a feisty old crust. Lots of energy. What energy? Rocket fuel. And Ms. Swille. She had a lawyer who could have sprung John Wilkes Booth. Lawyers for those who dwell in castles. The rich get off with anything, it's us serfs who have to pay. I don't want to be rich. Aunt Judy is right. I'm going to take this fifty rooms of junk and make something useful out of it.

Who pushed Swille into the fire? Some Etheric Double? The inexorable forces of history? A ghost? Thought? Or all of these? Who could have pushed him? Who?

"Uncle Robin?"

Robin turns to his secretary, Pompey, who as usual has appeared from out of nowhere.

"Yes, Pompey?"

"Raven is back!"

12:01 A.M.
Tamanaca Hotel, Room 127
Fat Tuesday
March 2, 1976
New Orleans

About the Author

ISHMAEL REED is the author of four previous novels, two books of poetry and numerous articles and reviews that have appeared in many publications. He is editor-in-chief of *Yardbird Reader* and director of Reed, Cannon and Johnson Communications. He has taught at the University of California in Berkeley and SUNY/Buffalo. Born in Chattanooga, Tennessee, he grew up in Buffalo and now lives in Berkeley with his wife, who is a dancer.